BARZAKH:
The Land In-Between

Barzakh: The Land In-Between

a novel

Moussa Ould Ebnou

Translated by Marybeth Timmermann

ISKANCHI
PRESS AND MAG

ISBN: 978-1-957810-00-3

Published in 2022 by Iskanchi Press
info@iskanchi.com
https://iskanchi.com/
+13852078509

Book Design (Cover and Text Layout)
by Ayebabeledaipre Sokari @ayeskreatif

Printed in the United States of America

Contents

Prelude

Teams from the Archaeological Institute of Human Thought were visiting tombs in search of buried vestiges of lost consciousnesses. This season, the excavations were taking place at Ghallawiya, in the northern part of Barzakh. Seventeen skeletons had already been excavated, at depths varying between seventy to one hundred meters below the surface, all in extremely poor condition. Usually, the bones crumbled into dust the moment they were unearthed, at the least breath of wind or the lightest touch of a brush. In this campaign, there remained only one more skeleton to extract, at the top of the mountain.

They dug down five meters to exhume it. It was isolated there, like an outlier, polished by the erosion of time, its skull crowned with fine, yellow sand. The archeologists bent over it with equal parts interest and perplexity, excited by their desire to read the thoughts of this being who just sprang out from the void.

The preliminary biocrystallographic tests revealed traces of Myelin in the form of solid crystals. Myelin crystals carry partial copies called "transcripts" which contain data on the speed, amplitude, and frequency of depolarization wave trains characterizing the activity of nerve cells. To unlock them, the crystals are simply dipped in an extremely concentrated aqueous solution of double-helix DNA. Once these transcripts are decoded, they can be translated into written sentences, thus expressing the flux of a consciousness during the typical phase of death throes.

Back in the lab at the Institute, the crystals were subjected to a physico-chemical analysis to identify partial copies. The transcripts were obtained and entered into the computer for syntactic and semantic decoding. A few moments later, a text started to scroll across the screen:

010/K73X7886B1C54EB1BBE83925BD015D19EF-78BENMS.Barzakh/Ghallawiya.T936.CP.D.123456789 10111213141516 1718... Memories of Vala had given way to a profound fear, a dreadful anguish and a ferocious hatred of the human species.

Part One

The Black Way

Prelude

Each hour that passed was torture for my body doomed to hunger and thirst, which abated at night only to make the trial more cruel the next day. Suffering gradually took over my entire body, like quicksand; my lips, mouth, and throat dried out and cracked. My stomach and intestines tightened up and were twisted by a prodigious force, as if wringing the last drops of liquid from them. A raging fire burned my entrails, the blaze spreading up my face, hands, and chest. Atrocious pain radiated throughout my entire body, getting worse over time, in sudden bursts, followed by slow lulls. My head and brain were painfully compressed by a powerful vice, and violent fits of fever racked my body, beginning with severe shivering, then despondency, then gradual euphoria. The intense pain eased up, the spasms stopped, and my legs stretched out. My panting, exhausted flesh no longer needed anything, no longer suffered, no longer felt hunger or thirst. The vultures approached me and put their rough feet with sharp claws on my body. When they struck me with their powerful beaks, my body shook in a violent convulsion. The vultures let go and leapt back, beating their huge, outstretched wings.

I heard a buzzing—impressions of chloroform through long sound waves. I was in a new world, where insignificant and bizarre memories of my departing life besieged me like vultures. As life was about to leave me, I felt like I was pulling away from my own body. At the same moment, a luminous tunnel appeared before me, and my past unfolded before my eyes. I had the feeling of reliving it, but this time, I witnessed it as a total stranger.

Throughout my existence, I have always tried in vain to connect my life to my dreams, my conscious to my unconscious, and my consciousness to other consciousnesses, so that I could judge others, myself, and time with a cool composure. But I remained isolated, a simple monad—adjusted, protected, and cut off from everything else. And suddenly, at the moment of my death, all these connections formed automatically with no effort on my part. In the throes of death, my dream and my life descended before me into the arena for an ultimate explanation, lining up in one very straight line, before sinking into the void. The entire world was piled up in a sort of little circular and transparent porthole, located just in front of me, where all enigmas and all secrets had come to be resolved, to become self-evident. The past, the present, and the future had merged into a single instant.

Dying had shed its unremitting light into every corner of my life. Laying bare everything I had touched. In that instant, I discovered the hidden meaning of situations, the significance of each silence, of every gesture and spoken word. Nothing about any being or thing escapes me now, not even their intentions. My entire life—so close, so inaccessible, and so inordinately gratuitous—is rewound and then replayed before me, a washed-up actor, an immobile spectator this time, tormented by the profound regret of having participated in this grotesque comedy.

The Salt Caravan

I remember that tragic night—I tossed and turned on my damp straw bed for hours, chasing an elusive night's sleep. I was tense, drenched in sweat, besieged by mosquitoes and macabre premonitions—terrible, nameless worries. Outside, it was oppressive. The heat had immobilized and solidified the air. I could still hear the muffled beating of distant drums that, for two days now, had been echoing endlessly across the entire savanna to announce the salt caravan. It was as if they were beating inside my head, which was on the verge of exploding. I could imagine the camel drivers entering into the enclosure reserved for the caravan, leading their animals—exhausted from the long and difficult journey— by the nose, and the slaves perched on the camels' backs, tirelessly beating the enormous drums securely wedged between the double loads. The caravan travelers would have their camels kneel while they unloaded their packsaddles, shouting to one another. The animals would be grunting and thrashing about in pain; the heavy loads they carried had bruised and scraped and dug into their backs for so long that necrosis had set in. The slabs of salt would be untied from the saddletrees, transported far from the fence and arranged in stacks, according to which merchant owned them. Once the camels were freed from their packsaddles, they would be led out of the enclosure and hobbled tightly to prevent them from wandering off. These desert men and beasts would be intoxicated by the strong smells of the luxurious vegetation of the African savanna and stunned by the oppressive heat so laden with humidity.

Dispassionate sleep had finally deigned to visit me when I felt a hand shake me vigorously and heard the voice of my father close to me.

"Gara! Gara! Wake up; get up, my son. We're going to the salt caravan. Hurry, hurry, before all the salt is sold!"

I squinted my eyes open—it was still dark out. I could hardly make out the silhouette of my father who was still shaking me. I got out of bed, rubbing my eyes, wobbly and half-asleep. My father put a rough calabash into my hands.

"Here, drink this. The day will be hot."

I lifted it to my mouth, gulping down the bitter mixture of water and curdled milk.

We left the village before dawn, passing the millet fields located to the west. I thought I was accompanying my father to comfort him during the trip. However, I was intrigued. In previous years, he went to the salt market with gold and slaves; now that he no longer had any slaves, he should have at least brought some gold.

"Father, how are we going to pay for the salt?"

"You'll see, it'll be easy! You merely have to ask one of the merchants to lend us some until the next caravan— I'll reimburse him with double the gold and double the slaves!"

The sun found us in a vast, marshy plain rich in aquatic plants and acacia trees whose sturdy branches supported thin, flexible stems that, after reaching their summit, fell back down in a tangle of richly flowering garlands. Often, they wound themselves around other nearby plants, becoming a tight unit with them through the interlacing, sinuous folds of their many branches, and forming a celestial vault through which other, still more beautiful compositions delighted the eyes.

The short shadows were still slightly slanted toward the west when we arrived in view of the marketplace. The slabs of salt sparkled in the sunlight; a dozen slaves put up for exchange were already there, surrounded by scattered piles of gleaming powdered gold, calabashes full of grain, heaps of multicolored fabric, elephant tusks, and a few horses. My father ordered me to go on ahead to wait for the salt merchants. Once I reached the marketplace, I stood next to the slaves and waited anxiously. The local Gangaras continued to parade about the marketplace. Each one set down his merchandise and ran back, in keeping with the long and ancient custom of silent trading between the Zenetes and the inhabitants of the gold country of the Sudanian savanna. This trade was carried out according to an immutable ceremony: the salt merchants, after traversing the Sahara and reaching the gold country, set up camp inside an enclosure formed by felled trees, and display the merchandise they have brought outside of the enclosure. On market day, the Gangaras arrive and take their turn to display the items they are offering in exchange, and then retire at a distance. If the merchants accept the proposed transaction, they take the items, leaving in their place their equivalency in salt, which the Gangaras would collect as soon as the Zenetes have left the marketplace. If, on the other hand, a salt merchant does not accept the proposed item, he takes his own merchandise back and the Gangara takes back his, unless he agrees to add a certain amount of gold to the already offered price.

Shortly after midday, the merchants came out of the enclosure and headed over to the marketplace in small groups. They were holding sharpened handsaws in their hands for cutting off portions of the salt slabs. A tall man with copper-colored skin approached me. He was wearing a short tunic— its fabric discolored by filth and faded by the sun— cinched around his waist with a wide leather belt falling over loosely gathered pants; a thick coil of rope hung from his right shoulder. He scrutinized every inch of me, from my head to my feet, with his gleaming, sunken eyes.

"My father, Fara Moul, asks if you would please lend him a bit of salt, until the next caravan, when he will repay you with double the gold and double the slaves!"

Perhaps the salt merchant was deaf—it was as if I hadn't

spoken. I repeated my father's request in a louder voice. He took a large slab of salt from the stack next to me and placed it at my feet. I got worried. In the caravan market, the salt slabs were cut out in the shape of the feet of the slave to be sold and the weight of that piece represented the price. He lifted my left foot and put it on the slab of salt and did the same with my right foot. I was now standing on it. He took his handsaw and cut off a chunk of salt following the contours of my feet. He then divided the rest of the salt into equal parts, took a canvas bag out from under his tunic, and gathered a few stacks of gold, putting salt in their place. He threw the sack of gold over his shoulder and took me by the arm, trying to take me toward the enclosure, but I managed to break free and, with a chunk of salt in my hands, ran toward my father. The merchant let out a terrible shout that echoed throughout the entire forest. They chased me down and caught me only a few hundred meters from the marketplace. I was taken back to the camp with a rope around my neck. They all joined in beating me soundly. Then, shackled like an animal, suffering from a thousand injuries, I was thrown in among the other slaves in the corner of the enclosure.

The caravan broke camp that same day. That year, they had sold almost all their salt; only a few slabs remained, and they would be sold off at stopovers along the return route. Black men dressed like the Zenetes and speaking their language helped the merchants load up the packsaddles and put them on the animals. The camels reserved for baggage carried wooden saddletrees, made from two connecting arches joined together by two braces; each arch was comprised of a pair of opposing slats, doweled together two by two and placed on top of the thick rolls of padding, which were folded in half in front of the hump. An anchor rope was tied to a collar whose rings held a curved piece of wood placed between the arches, serving as surcingle, girth strap, and crupper all at the same time. Tied off to one side of the collar, it went under the animal's belly, behind the sternal callus, came back to pass through the curve of the wooden arch, looped around the camel's neck and then under its tail and over its back to finally return and be tied off at the collar. A few other camels carried tri-lobed saddles, with tall flat pommels, cantle backrests, and raised panels, made with pieces of wood and leather that were fitted, doweled, nailed, sewn, or laced together. The saddle was held in place by a strap affixed to the saddletree band and by a crupper made of braided leather, passing under the camel's tail to prevent the saddle from tipping forward.

The caravan men shouted to make the camels kneel, get up, or calm down. They verified that the reins were properly tied to the metal rings placed in the right nostril of certain camels, tightening the chin strap around the lower jaw of others, or hobbled the knees of some nervous beast who might try to stand up. Then, they loaded the baggage. The great rectangular goatskin or sheepskin sacks, beautifully decorated in many bright colors, predominantly red, dangled from long ropes tied to the saddles in front of the pommels. Other larger and heavier sacks were placed on the pack camel's flanks, securely attached to the saddletrees. They hung the goatskins up by their legs—swollen and dripping with milk or butter—balanced equally on both sides of the camels. Finally, they untied the hobbles and made the camels stand up one by one. And the caravan started off. A few men rode in the saddles, but most of them walked, pulling the camels by their bridles. The newly acquired slaves had their hands tied to the end of a rope attached to a saddle or saddletree and walked painfully to the side and back of their new masters' camels. Some, unable to walk, were dragged along the ground. I was amongst those. I stumbled and tripped with each step. When I fell, I was pulled along the ground. Thorns dug into my face, chest, stomach, and legs. Sometimes I managed to get up and walk painfully. Then the camel's urine—which always sprayed backwards—would hit me in the face and get in my eyes and mouth as it was spattered by the wind.

The caravan crossed hills covered in greenery, separated by numerous valleys full of luxurious vegetation. The woods were inhabited by wild boars and antelope. The yowls of a wild cat who had caught sight of the caravan could be heard before it slipped away. The hilltops, peaks blazing in the red light of the setting sun, poured out their exaggerated shadows across the valley floors already devoured by the encroaching night. The caravan halted near a pond surrounded by gigantic baobab trees. Some of them had neither branches nor leaves, and in spite of that, their trunks were thicker than several trees together. Some had suffered from a decay that had left holes in them and might provide a happy alternative to the muddy pond water, for those cavities often held rainwater for a long time. They might also be inhabited by some spinning creature who had set up her weaving shop there or by bees buzzing around a hive bursting with honey. But this particular evening, the men of the caravan found a decomposing cadaver there, still wrapped in its burial shroud— tradition called for burying griots inside the hollows of baobab trees. Swarms of buzzing mosquitoes stuck to my skin, causing abominable pain. I was still hobbled, but I forgot my suffering and fell into a deep sleep. I saw myself in the sky holding a comet by its tail. This image, the only one I remembered after I woke up, intrigued me for a long time. My master woke me up before dawn to prepare for our departure. A big fire was already lit in the middle of the camp and the caravan men were shouting and running back and forth between the baggage and the animals. The caravan set off again, heading toward the north. At dawn, we crossed a stream with a fast current. The water came up to the men's necks and soaked the dromedaries' bellies. Downstream, not far from where we crossed, men were crossing in the opposite direction with tall earthenware jars on their heads.

A burning wind from the east picked up and the heat was overwhelming by mid-morning. The caravan had to halt before noon, setting up camp under a huge baobab near the entrance to a village. This was where passing travelers traditionally rested while they waited for the villagers to come offer their hospitality. As the caravan watched, women came out with gourds full of millet, sour milk, cooked chickens, lotus flour, and beans. The men of the caravan bought what they wanted with little pieces of rock salt. A man, even whiter than the Zenetes and wrapped in a dirty pagne, came up to the caravan with his Sudanese guide. The furtive look in his clear blue eyes revealed an unhealthy curiosity. He seemed completely out of place and his presence was an unspoken threat. He spoke in an unfamiliar language and his guide translated.

"My name is al-Nacrani, and I would like to join your caravan to go to Awdaghost. I have learned from travelers that in that city, you can find young women with beautiful faces, fair skin, supple bodies, perky breasts, small waists, broad shoulders, ample behinds, and narrow vaginas. They assured me that whoever is lucky enough to have one will experience as much pleasure as with a virgin in Paradise."

Al-Nacrani accepted polite greetings from the caravan men, who invited him to join them. This man had the appetite of a black hole. He kept asking for sanglé—a local soup that he had taken a voracious passion for—which was a sort of thick mush prepared with an herb similar to cocoyam. Every time he was given some, he would ask for more as if his stomach had no limits. On that particular day, the men of the caravan had bought a large quantity of it, so there was enough for everyone to have as much as they wanted. Al-Nacrani and the slaves drank a significant amount of it. A few hours later, they were all sick. Several lost consciousness during the afternoon prayer. The caravan men solicited a remedy from a village healer, who brought a vomit-inducing substance made out of pulverized plant roots mixed with anise and sugar that he put into water and shook. Those who were sick drank this medicine and vomited everything they had eaten along with a lot of yellow bile. One of the slaves died. After washing him and wrapping him up in a white burial shroud, the men of the caravan recited the ritual death prayers for him. Then they took the body to be buried in a nearby cemetery, near the entrance of the village.

"Hurry up; we are going to load up the baggage and leave," cried the caravan chief to the slaves who carried the body.

The animals were already loaded up and were about to stand up when the village chief made his way over to the caravan, accompanied by an imposing entourage and surrounded by men armed with sabers and lances. The warriors formed a circle around the caravan. The chief brandished his saber wrathfully, his cheeks and lips trembling.

"Why have you miserable foreigners dared to offend our dead?"

The caravan men's eyes grew wide and they stared at the chief, his entourage and his soldiers, and then looked at each other. No one understood the reason for this anger. Finally, Taluthane, the chief of the caravan, came forward.

"Noble Chief, how can you level such a serious accusation against our peaceful caravan who were enjoying your generous hospitality?"

"Are you that miserable, that you thank us for our hospitality?"

"I beg of you, tell me what you reproach us for!"

"You have committed a heinous crime. You have offended the spirits of our dead!"

"But how could we have done that?"

"You buried the body of a slave among them!"

"But what's wrong with that?"

"It's a crime! Slaves are buried in cemeteries reserved for them, far from the cemeteries for free men. The spirits of the slaves must not trouble the spirits of their masters!"

"I humbly beg your pardon, honorable Chief! We were unaware of this custom—for us, men are equal in death. But we will immediately dig up the body and put it in the slave cemetery."

"That is not enough! You must give us a slave to be sacrificed, to appease the spirits of our dead."

Taluthane designated one of his slaves for the sacrifice and the village chief ordered his soldiers to grab him. As they took him toward the village square, he tried to resist, screaming horribly, like a beast whose throat is being cut. The exhumed cadaver was transported to the appropriate cemetery.

The sky had darkened to the east, thunder rumbled from the threatening storm, and the flashes of lightning irrigating the sky indicated that it was close. A lead wall advanced, melding the sky with the earth. Then it unleashed a violent wind that swept up clouds of sand that whipped the body and carried off everything in their way. Later, the wind eventually died down and the storm dissipated without a drop of rain. When the caravan finally left the village, the dust had settled, and the air had resumed its immobile transparency. A full moon lit up the sky. The men walked in front and to the side of their beasts and behind them in a line.

After two hours of painful trekking, al-Nacrani, his tattered pagne dragging behind, launched into a litany of complaints, hoping to wrest compassion from the caravan men; he hopped from one to another, begging each one to let him ride on his camel. But the animals were already overloaded and tired; they could not bear any more weight. Al-Nacrani kept on badgering everyone.

"I'm exhausted," he said, "my feet and legs are bloody. I can't walk any longer!"

Not only was he unused to walking, but he was also handicapped by the impressive amount of sanglé he had ingested. His pleading was in vain. Some responded that through this suffering, and with resignation, he would gain entrance to paradise, which he took as sarcasm. Others told him that in Awdaghost, everything would be forgotten. Finally, giving up on camels, he made a deal with one of the slaves to be carried on his back, in exchange for three tobacco leaves.

In the dim moonlight, the path was very difficult and the slave who carried al-Nacrani got many thorns stuck in his feet. He was forced to stop often to pull out the biggest ones. During these stops, al-Nacrani remained securely on his back to save himself the bother of having to get off and then on again. The slave advanced with difficulty, sweating profusely, and panting like a sickly beast. Since he was bored, al-Nacrani attempted to make small talk with his ride.

"Is this the first time you are on the caravan?"

There was no response from his ride, who was huffing and puffing. When the terrain got a bit easier, he panted his response. "M... y master... Zenk... Zenko Ba... Zenko Bada... exchanged me for salt... Be... fore... I work... ed... in his tob... acco field..."

Al-Nacrani had already stopped listening. His face lifted to the sky, he gazed at the great curve of light formed by the Milky Way. In the brightest part of this milky belt that crossed the entire sky, Sagittarius let his arrow fly as the three summer beauties watched. All around, the black veil was studded with an infinite number of diamonds, and the night went by at its steady rhythm, creating the illusion that it left beings well enough alone. The calm was barely troubled by the panting beasts and the rustling grass under their feet.

In a loud voice, one of the men in the caravan sang out the call to the morning prayer. The convoy stopped without kneeling the animals. The sky grew incandescent in the east, and a great flame rose up from the horizon, chasing everyone from the empyrean, which was soon deserted by the stars frantically rushing off. Alone, holding close to the moon in the desert sky, the Shepherd's Star resisted for a moment against the dragon's fire, before vanishing soon after with her knight, snatched up by the sun.

Taluthane

The fields of cotton and millet were rippling in the valley breeze. A nearby village was waking up to its Sisyphean labor. The doorways into the little round huts with straw roofs and the makeshift shacks made from mats stitched together were so low that the only way to enter them was by crawling. The little groups of straw huts were surrounded by enclosures of living bushes planted haphazardly or by fences made of straw. Sometimes, the enclosures were nothing but simple stakes. The extremely narrow streets were winding and dirty. Women and children milled around between the huts and in the courtyards teeming with fowl. The men came out of the village heading toward the fields, and dogs barked at the caravan. In the nearby stream, fishermen used wooden cudgels to stun the fish and then string them up on the ropes suspended from posts jutting out of the water.

The caravan halted toward the middle of the day, when the heat got too oppressive. Camp was pitched in the shade of the usual baobab and merchants came out with their provisions. A noisy crowd was making a commotion in the village courtyard. They were stoning a young bride because her wedding night did not find her on "God's path." This young beauty's hair hung in braids and she wore golden jewels on her forehead. Her dowry was displayed in the courtyard to be admired and appreciated by all, but one crucial piece was missing—there was no "virginity cloth."

Al-Nacrani's ride had collapsed in the middle of the double loads, exhausted and dead-tired. His master left him in peace; he had gotten his share of tobacco. Al-Nacrani was giving this under-employed slave the opportunity to make a profit for the whole length of the journey. A teenager was playing *diara la kassi* with a piece of carved wood attached to the end of a long cord, vigorously swinging his bullroarer through the air to make a sort of roaring sound. I also knew how to "make the lion roar." Only ten days ago, I had graduated to the *big cats* of my village. To move from *little cat* to *big cat*, you had to pass a harsh test. The *little cats* lined up in two rows, and each one had to pass through the double column and endure a whipping from his comrades. Anyone who flinched or walked too quickly was not allowed into the upper class. I had successfully passed the test. My confidence had impressed the jury of graduating *big cats*, who, before leaving us in charge, revealed to us the group's secret by teaching us how to spin the bullroarer.

Once I had graduated into the *big cats*, I shed the shorts of my childhood—a worn strip of cotton fabric wound between my legs and held up at the waist by a string—and started wearing new shorts with matching ribbons of animal hide on either side and a wide band flowing over my lower back. This attire authorized me to claim my place among the young masters in the village courtyard. But now, I have been kidnapped by the caravan. The lovely ribbons on my new shorts were filthy and ragged. The village and its *big cats* got farther away every day. In every village the caravan passed through, there were the *little cats*, the *big cats*, the young men who ruled the village courtyard, the established notables, and the old men who watched the eras lapping against the shores of eternity… At any moment, anyone could be ripped out of the ordinary rhythm of life and taken away on the long road of the caravan.

When the sun started to set, loosening its grip on the already wistful earth, we brought back the camels and led them through the corridor formed by the two rows of half-loads that had already been lined up. Then we had them kneel in front of the corresponding load. Once the saddlepacks were on and loaded up, we had them stand up, and the caravan started off again. A few villagers gathered around to watch it move off.

The lead camel, a massive ash-gray gelding, belonged to Taluthane, the leader of the caravan. He was a Zenete from Awdaghost and a wealthy trader with a dozen other camels in the convoy. The lead camel was led by Chi Baro, the caravan guide. This Gangara, from the Tambaoura Valley, appeared to be as timeless as his smooth animal hide vest. His limping gait was a result of a birth defect that caused his left leg to be slightly shorter than his right one. He lived in

Awdaghost, at the very edge of the Great Desert, and offered his services to the caravans for a half slab of salt for each round-trip journey.

Taluthane had sold all his salt and was returning with a lot of gold and good slaves. He walked along stroking his long black beard and looking preoccupied. Sometimes he was in the lead, near Chi Baro, and sometimes he fell back to the middle of the convoy. Before he had left, he had learned that his wife, whom he suspected was being unfaithful to him, received visits from a lover each time he was gone. *Yet, how languorous and full of despair she seemed when we said goodbye! She stood for a long time in the doorway, all dressed up, her gauzy garments partially open and her belt loosened around her narrow waist. Her moist eyes made her face irresistibly sensual as she murmured dulcet words of longing and regret.*

The more the husband thought about these parting images, the more unhappy he became. It made him forget about his salt, his gold, his slaves, the hardships of travel, and even his own breathing. But this time he was resolved to get to the bottom of it. *I will not leave again until I have figured out the truth. I will take every necessary measure. A few weeks after my return, I will announce that I'm going to undertake a long journey. Once my preparations are complete, I will leave with a few companions, but once we get to the first stopover, I will leave them on the pretext of a matter that requires me to return home. When I get close to home, I will hide my camel and my weapons and I will approach in secret to see what is happening in my house. I'll climb the wall and thus be able to see in without being discovered.*

He imagined he would see his wife with her lover. They would be bathed in a soft light amid the swirling smoke of incense. They would be scantily clad and, with her delicate hands tangled in his curly hair, she would be holding his head against her bosom. He would have proof of the misfortune he had feared. He would immediately go back and arm himself, mount his camel, and return to the house.

My arrival will spread fear, and, while she hides the lover in one room, I will enter looking indifferent and give her a plausible reason to justify my return. She will believe me and bring me something to eat. After she serves me supper, I will tell her to bring out the guest she was entertaining.

"Do I have a guest?"

"Yes! You have one and he is there in that room!"

She will continue to deny the fact, but I will get up and drag the man out of the room, telling him to come dine with us.

He will respond, "Alas, I'm not hungry! To deliver me from this disgrace, I ask for death!"

I will then tell him, "Come now, there is no harm done; better people than you have succumbed to temptation!"

At my insistence, he will decide to join us at the table and after the meal is finished, I will send him off without mistreating him, giving him a disguise to wear as he leaves.

Then I will say to my wife, "Don't worry about what just happened here—other women before you have made mistakes and have given in to their passions. There are very few people who can resist temptation! So, I will keep this affair secret and even give it a twist that you will like. Since I am perfectly sure that nothing could have led you astray or driven you to act in this way except the irresistible power of love, I will allow you to marry your lover, satisfy your passion, and live with him publicly, without compromising yourself. But with the following condition: after spending an entire year with him, you will send for me so that I can pass by and see you in plain view of your husband. You will come out for me to see you all dressed up, with all your charms on display. You will tell me about your husband and you will complain about his bad behavior. Jealousy will drive him to renounce you, and I will once again become your husband as before. In this way, you will have satisfied your passion and, in choosing me over your seducer, you will put an end to any suggestions of impotence that might fall on me."

I am certain that her lover would be bad-tempered. Perhaps he would even beat her often. But she will agree to everything, still only seeing his good sides. So, I will send for her father and the rest of her family. Then, after offering them a meal, I will ask them to ask my wife how I have treated her and how it was when we lived together. She will respond by praising me and saying that I had always treated her with respect and kindness. Then, at my invitation, they will ask her to say if she wants to stay with me.

"No," she will say. "I no longer want him. His absence is more pleasant to me than his presence. I have searched my heart for the strength to stay with him, but it has led me elsewhere and much too far to allow for a reconciliation between us. He can renounce me and I will release him from all his obligations toward me!"

I will show an extreme desire to keep her, but before the end of the discussion, I will agree to an arrangement. We will agree that she will become her own person and that I will be completely released from all my contractual obligations toward her. Her parents will thank me for my generosity and, addressing my wife, will blame her for the whole thing. As soon as she is free to contract a second marriage, she will marry her lover who will be the first to ask for her hand. She will live with him for a year and will find that time drags on, for she will realize that I was much worthier than her new husband. And at the end of the year, she will not forget to fulfill her promise to me. When she invites me over, I will be on my way, and the moment I pass by her house, she will come out, wearing a dress that shows off her curves and puts all her charms on display...

Brooding over his jealousy, Taluthane had lost the rhythm of the caravan's pace and found himself far behind. The moon was already high in the sky, and although the stars were few and far between, those few shone all the more gloriously. He was walking slowly, his head down, smoothing his beard which seemed to grow longer with every caress.

...Her gauzy dress will reveal all her charms. She will start to lament the behavior of her second husband and will wag her finger at him. He will go mad with jealousy, get up and fatally wound her with a stab of his lance. The brothers and parents of the victim will pounce on the assassin and take his life. Thus, I will be avenged and rid of that slut and her lover, without having dirtied my hands with the red liquid that flows in their veins and their arteries and that carries their waste! Or maybe, when the caravan is only one day from Awdaghost, I will harness a riding camel that is silent and speedy, and I will enter the town just after nightfall while no one expects us until the late afternoon of the next day at the earliest. I will kneel the camel behind the house and enter furtively. He will be there, hungrily

kissing her neck, her hands clutching the muscles of his back, and they will be in their own world. I will go past them without stopping and will simply say, almost to myself, "What could he possibly see in her to make him love her so much?" My words will break the charm, and the troubled stream of the outside world will again flood into the torpid senses of the lovers who, in a panic will reach for their damp and wrinkled clothing, frantically grabbing at their tangled underclothes scattered across the room. I will have dinner served to me by my favorite slave and will retire to sleep alone.

Or maybe, if the lover turns out to be that young man who works for us, that visionary from Aratane who looks like Christ, I will leave one or two days after our return, on the pretext of doing an errand on horseback, and, after letting myself fall from the saddle, I will be carried back to the house complaining that I can't move my legs or my arms. My wife will come and take care of me and will stay near me for part of the night. Then, I will pretend to be overcome with sleep and will remain motionless, like a person who has fainted. Seeing me like this, she will leave my room to go meet up with her seducer in the service courtyard, but I will follow her and listen to them. The Christ of Aratane will tell her, "It took you so long to come, and you left me with no supper!" To which she will respond, "My duties to that man kept me far from you, but do not reproach me, for you are the beloved of my heart and he is nothing but the father of my children!"

Without betraying my presence, I will return to my bed. But, at the first sign of danger, when the call to arms rings out, and when everyone is rushing to push the enemy back, I will take up my weapons, mount my horse, and order the Christ and the other servants to follow my example. When we find ourselves in front of the enemy, I will tell the seducer to charge ahead and that I will follow him. Since he will *have to obey, he will run into the midst of the enemy. Then I will turn right around and abandon him to his fate. He will be the first to fall in battle. No one will suspect that it was an act of vengeance.*

When she sees me coming home, she will cry out, "Praise be to God who brought you back safe and sound!"

I will reply, "That's nice, but the beloved of your heart is neither safe nor sound, whereas I am nothing but the father of your children."

She will recognize her own words and know that I heard her entire conversation with the Christ. She will beg me to send her back to her family and I will agree.

He stopped on a ridge to relieve his bladder. The earth had already put on its great white robe for a new celebration of the sun. The pale lemon-yellow liquid frothed when it hit the thin black crust that covered the ground, forming a hole around the point of impact that got wider and deeper; some spilled over the edge and just missed splashing onto his left foot and shoe—a light, open sandal made of oryx hide with two heel straps padded on the inside and the hole between the toes reinforced with a metallic ring— but the flow was already ebbing. He picked up a dead twig and straightened up, wiping off the last few droplets that were still slowly dripping out. He lifted his head and looked toward the northwest, opening his eyes wide to take in the entire expanse of the immobile landscape. In a few moments, when everything would be flooded by the swift waves of the brilliant sunlight, his major oblique muscles would contract and his pupils would contract to survey things from wisely half-closed eyelids.

He had fallen behind the caravan. The last camels were at the top of a hill and then disappeared with the men down the opposite slope. He picked up his pace to catch up with the convoy. He joined us down in the valley, in the middle of the last prostration of morning prayer and took his place at the far right of the line. I was also praying. I managed to go through the ritual movements without suffering too much, as I was now used to my wounds and the pain they caused. I would have been happy to skip the prayers, having no affection for this religion; after all, my discovery of it had coincided with my misfortune. But my master forced me to pray each time and was quick to beat me if I wasn't attentive enough. So, I went through the motions mechanically and without conviction. Sometimes, when the men seemed absorbed in their fervent poses, my gaze would stray from the direction of Mecca and fall upon al-Nacrani's hooked nose and nasty curled lip.

At the hottest point of the day, when pupils were contracted to the maximum due to the glare from the waves gliding through the grass that swayed to the rhythm of the wind, Chi Baro looked for a place to rest and drink. He drew up to the immobile shadow of the usual huge baobab near the entrance to Sama. In this village, the men went about absolutely naked and the women, who all had shaved heads, wore only braided leather thongs covering their sexual parts. Among the women who came out to sell provisions to the caravan, there was a curvaceous girl with wide eyes who seemed to pay particular attention to Taluthane. When her companions had left, she came and stood before him and spoke a few words. Taluthane called for Chi Baro to serve as interpreter. She repeated the words without looking away from her chosen one's face. Then suddenly a euphoric expression transformed the guide's face, and he clapped his left hand over his mouth to stop the irrepressible burst coming up his throat and, since it found no outlet through his mouth, was held back in a suppressed snort and then came back out through his eyes, in glistening tears of laughter.

"Well, what does she want?" demanded Taluthane.

Chi Baro—failing to suppress his laughter—translated, "She wants to have your beard on the only part of her body that is not exposed to view!"

"What does that mean? Speak, you wretch! How dare this black woman insult me in this way?"

Chi Baro was still snorting and was now holding his face in both hands and shaking with laughter. Then, seeing the Zenete's violent anger, he said, "It is a custom here. The women shave their heads but never their pubis. Here the length of their pubic hair is an important criteria for beauty."

This explanation, instead of calming Taluthane, made him angrier still. He raised his stick threateningly at the immodest girl and shouted insults at her. He ran after her and she tried to escape him by running between the rows of half-loads. They chased each other around the baobab tree several times. The Zenete was about to catch her when she tripped on one of the tie-down ropes and fell down between two large sacks. Taluthane threw himself on top of her, after which only cries, curses, gasps, and giggles could be heard. When they finally got up, they were out of breath and unsteady on their feet. Sweat and dust trickled from their exhausted bodies; one shook the dust from his beard while the other adjusted her tangled leather thong, and the Zenete's anger seemed appeased. The others were no longer watching and had returned to the drowsiness of their siesta. Nearby, the occasional animal still roamed. Old friends with the light, the camels had knelt in their own shadows, faces to the sun, while the herds of cattle, sheep, and goats huddled in the middle of the deepest shadows. Inside the huts, poultry and dogs had already reached the boiling point.

Toward the end of the afternoon, when the dromedaries casually got up to leave again, the young women of the village followed the caravan for a moment, performing the river dance. Running along the vast fields of millet stretching out to the right, the narrow path made a deep scar that was overrun by vegetation. The new slaves, still tied up and pulled along by ropes knotted securely to the pommels of the saddles or the arches of the saddletrees, followed off to the side, to the right or left of the beasts. My wrists were tied with rope again. A useless precaution—I was so exhausted and full of despair that I no longer had the strength to dream of escaping. I stumbled on the plump seed heads that overflowed onto the path. The still unstable loads sought their point of equilibrium like balancing scales, with the men of the caravan watching them closely and running here and there to make adjustments one way or another, without impeding the march of the convoy. Later, when they would be stabilized and the pack camels settled into their cruising speed, the men of the caravan would no longer worry about the convoy and would be able to take their time, lagging far behind, singing and dreaming of far distant ports. Or, like this smoker, undo the knots of the leather string on his tobacco pouch and lay it out flat on his left hand, taking out his engraved bone and copper pipe and running the pipe-cleaner through it before blowing away the leftover burned tobacco, then crushing a bit of tobacco taken from his tobacco pouch, packing the pipe by pressing the tobacco down with his right index finger, taking out the amadou tinder, the flint, and the striker or *znad*, pinching a little clump out of the ball of organic fiber, holding it between his thumb and index finger, and drawing the striker sharply across the flint to make a spark that sets the fiber on fire, placing the fiber into the pipe with the pointed end of the striker, and breathing in deeply for the first time. The strong taste of the *karkriya* tobacco, harvested under the palm trees of Lemtouna Mountain, would radiate from his lungs to his brain, numbing his entire body for a moment. Columns of purified white smoke would come out through his nostrils and our torture would be made even more unbearable. But for now, they still had to balance the half-loads, tighten up the tie-downs, replace any frayed ropes, lead the reluctant beasts, and whip us. And to think that it was a beautiful day! Our pupils reflected the light blue of the sky, so deep, our gazes drowning between the few cumulus clouds floating in the distance like inaccessible life preservers. Gusts of warm humid air passed over the caravan without slowing, then died out over the middle of the fields. The great heat of the day was starting to peter out.

The smoker breathed in a second time and swallowed the smoke, holding the pipe between his crooked, nicotine-covered teeth.

"Pass me the pipe," repeated the man who had been walking beside him for a while.

When he passed it to him, the tobacco had already burned completely up and its bitter smoke was full of tar.

The shadows that had crept cowardly into their shells, playing dead in the hottest part of the day, now shamelessly stretched out to take possession of the earth. Barely mourning the day, they were already embracing each other in a silent celebration of the night. While the birds, in an agitated tumult, performed the last complicated patterns of flight on their way to their nests, the men picked up their pace, glancing around furtively. The smoker with crooked teeth now walked in front. A shiver passed over my back and up my neck. Invisible presences emerged from all sides, eager to take their place in the night. Things had shed their familiar masks, taking on strange appearances and suddenly coming alive.

The great baobab of Iresni sheltered us for the night. The

moon had not yet risen and only Chi Baro's experience, quickly confirmed by the first fires and a chorus of ferocious barking, had led us to our stopover. We unloaded the camels and lit a big fire for light and to drive off the mosquitoes. Some women brought out a few meager provisions. Mush and sour milk were purchased. The camels, tightly hobbled, writhed around and jostled each other, tormented by the mosquitoes. I was exhausted, hungry, and thirsty. My master gave me a bowl of milk that I drank down in one gulp. After the endless chores, I fell into the deep sleep of a beast of burden.

We didn't leave Iresni until after sunrise. The village and the surrounding area were drowning in an ocean of light. The herds were already out and a few lingering nanny goats were rubbing themselves up against the trees, dreaming of billy goats. The caravan glided through the dazzling light which seemed to have the consistency of water. When I turned around to avoid being sprayed in the face by camel urine, which burned my eyes, I noticed the red eyes of the new slave who was walking behind me. Bitter tears mingled with the urine dripped from his impassive face. Later, a providential wind picked up and redirected the urine toward the front, sparing our faces.

The route wound around a small mountain. The entrance to a cavern was visible on the southern slope where multicolored pieces of cloth were suspended over a bower of foliage behind which, as we advanced toward the northeast, a stone house with a rounded roof appeared. Men came out of it carrying bowls and large vases that they placed in front of the entrance to the cavern. Their strange whistling echoed throughout the valley in sonorous waves. Suddenly, the mane of a dragon with a camel's head appeared in the entrance to the cavern. But the mountain slipped behind us off to our right, and the southern slope disappeared to gradually make room for the northwestern slope.

At Ghiyaru, the caravan was welcomed by a certain Abu Mussa, an Ibadi expatriate originally from Djerid, who had settled in this town long ago. He had been passing through when he first arrived, but upon discovering his passion for the courageous and energetic locals, who went around naked and led such a simple life, he decided to stay there forever. Ever since, he'd been taking part in the gold harvest and the raids that the Ghiyaru people made into the country of the Lamlams where they took captives and sold them off in Ghana and in Awdaghost. He came out to greet the caravan, on the other side of the ditch that surrounded the town, accompanied by slaves carrying drinks and food. The next day, he came along with us for a considerable distance away from the village before saying goodbye to the caravan. He had tears in his eyes and his voice faltered from the nostalgia he felt for the long course of the caravan. I dared not suggest that he take my place.

Forests of arak and argan trees were interspersed all along the road between Ghiyaru and Samakanda. Near this last village, we saw several archers practicing on the fruits of these trees. They were particularly talented, their arrows piercing the ironwood fruit which were about the size and shape of dates. Beyond Samakanda stretched a long prairie leading toward Ghana. When I realized I was coming as a slave to this city that had always fascinated me, I could only curse fate which seemed to assail me so relentlessly.

At our last stopover before Ghana, my master woke me up during the night. I was exhausted and had only just fallen asleep. He had a hard time waking me up, so he began to kick and insult me. I only emerged from the depths of my slumber after a bucket of cold water was thrown in my face. The sky had darkened in the east; bolts of lightning were flashing— a storm threatened. The slaves had already dug large holes where they were stowing the merchandise to preserve it from the rain. I started to dig a hole for my master's merchandise while he continued to berate me. How I would have loved to bury him in that hole instead of the merchandise! Everyone took off their clothes to put them in with the merchandise before burying them. We were all completely naked, masters as well as slaves, just like at birth. The rain came down in torrents for a good part of the night. It was very cold. When it stopped, we dug up the merchandise and the clothing, which had stayed dry. We lit a fire, which took a long time to catch in the soaked wood. The comforting sun finally rose, wrapping us in its heat and making us forget the wind and rain of the night.

The prairie was smoking. Faint steam was rising from everywhere, attracted by the sun. Here and there, in front of the huts and in the fields, thick white columns swirled and rose up in wispy tendrils, like evil spirits escaping from their bottles. One mounted slave started crying out, "Ghana! Ghana!"

For a while, I could make nothing out; then as I peered through the steam, which was now dissipating, I saw the first minarets dancing. And then, I counted a dozen of them performing complicated movements to the rhythm of our march. At the gates to the city, we were stopped by soldiers and the king's tax collectors. They counted our pack camels, verified the contents of our loads, and calculated the taxes to be paid by the caravan. I called out to a group of soldiers passing next to me, "Help! Help! Help me! I was kidnapped when I went to get salt for my father!"

One of the soldiers hit me violently with his spear handle, ordering me to shut up. After having paid off its taxes in gold and in salt, the caravan was allowed to enter into the city. We were on the right bank of the river that flowed through the city. Sprawling neighborhoods in the southern outskirts consisted of shanties, straw huts, and round huts made of branches or dry stones. Deafening swarms of naked children arrived from every direction and followed the caravan, throwing rocks at the bound slaves. I received a few of them, and to avoid the others, I lowered my head and positioned myself between the pelvic limbs of the camel, swaying between its thighs to the rhythm of its steps. A young woman with a large calabash on her head walked quickly alongside and called out to me as she looked for my face between the camel's thighs, "Millet, catjang, chicken!"

Then, the caravan crossed a neighborhood with tall houses made of stone blocks. To the left, on the other side of the river, a palace stood right in the middle of the forest. The lead camels had left the riverbank and were disappearing between the houses toward the right; the rest of the caravan followed. I, in turn, entered the narrow, winding street, hemmed in between the tall, windowless houses with raised doorsteps. I no longer saw anything in front of me except two camels and the tail of the third which disappeared to the left almost immediately; the head of the second one disappeared in the same direction, followed by its neck, body, and hind legs. Then the camel pulling me was swallowed up in turn. I ended up in a vast, open area teeming with shops and market stalls. The lead camels of the caravan were already kneeling. Another convoy was leaving to the northeast. Exhausted, I collapsed without even waiting for them to untie me from the camel. But the master came and kicked me until I got up. I was led along with the new slaves into an enclosed courtyard surrounded by a high wall, where we were piled up into small huts. Giants armed with sabers and lances kept a close watch on us.

We stayed for three weeks in Ghana, during which we were cared for and well fed, "getting us ready to be displayed at the market in Awdaghost," said some apparently well-informed slaves. Then, one day, our guards let us out of the huts and brought us to the village square where the loaded camels were already standing and the caravan was ready for a new departure. I was tied up once again with the same rope, behind the same camel.

Awdaghost

We were at our tenth stopover after Ghana, preparing to load up the baggage before sunrise, to be at Awdaghost before the midday heat. The unsullied dawn hastily unveiled the face of the earth, unceremoniously disturbing the slumber of life. Beings and things began to stir in a Zoroastrian murmur and the eastern horizon burst into light. Suddenly, about thirty men riding beautiful horses, armed with eight to ten-foot lances, swords, and daggers, raced down the nearby hillside in a cloud of dust. For a brief instant, wild hope—which only perishes with life itself— made me think that this furious gang was going to massacre the men of the caravan and that I would be able to take advantage of the confusion to escape and return to Ghana. But the caravan leader, with abundant salutations and exaggerated reverences, took one of the sacks containing powdered gold and offered it to the leader of the gang. The gang leader opened the sack, caressed, weighed, and sniffed at the powdered gold and, apparently satisfied with the gift, made a sweeping motion with his arm, ordering his men to retreat. The gang disappeared as fast as they had arrived. I felt the pain of my shackles even more cruelly. And so dissipated the glimmer of hope, more ephemeral than the dust kicked up by the horses. When the caravan could set off again, the sun was already showing the edge of its crown.

Lazy shadows from rocky stumps lay across the path, caressing the stretches of smooth sand. Short, abrupt sounds, seemingly closer and closer, bounced and echoed from one stump to the next, like nimble hunters lying in wait. They intrigued me at first, but when I saw a man hack into a trunk with his ax, I understood that they were cutting down trees all throughout the valley. In the long, wooded corridors, between the swells of dunes, the trees trembled at the sound of the axes, but remained in place, tethered to the earth, incapable of fleeing from the approaching danger. Countless herds of sheep, cattle, and camels were grazing or clumped together around the wells that were becoming more and more frequent.

Before midday, the caravan arrived within eyesight of the tall, white hill that overlooked Awdaghost. The call announcing the caravan was passed from watch post to watch post all along the southern part of the rocky ring encircling the city. And here they were under the clouds: the towering minarets of Awdaghost, rising up proudly as conquerors of the sky, and, in the broad arena filled with blazing eyes, the ocher smile of its majestic abodes slumbering in the shadows of their gardens.

The city was nestled in a great basin closed off by a very uneven grouping of rocks. The heat was even more oppressive here because the air all around was filled with a strong smoke odor. Great columns of thick smoke rose up from a neighborhood to the southeast that clung to an overhang of the cliff. The square for caravans opened up by a rather high door to allow for mounted camel riders to pass through. The beasts were upset by the clamor and movements of a large crowd. The master, who was taking off my shackles, shouted something at me that I couldn't hear because of the deafening din from the nearby stalls. He grabbed my arm violently and took me to a camel that was still loaded.

After being nourished and cared for, I found myself on display with the others in the marketplace. The market attracted a large part of the population of Awdaghost and many visitors from the surrounding areas: curious onlookers, bargain hunters, blacksmiths looking for leather and precious metals, their raw material; traffickers of all kinds, slave merchants, word seekers, panhandling griots with forked tongues, sorcerers, vendors selling talismans and amulets for protection (against weapons, devils, curses, etc.) or for propitiation (to be happy in love or to be successful in business); marabouts, preachers, and streetwalkers with long legs and curvaceous rumps. An assorted crowd of all races and all colors jostled together, including Muslim women in veils covering everything but their eyes, exuberant Sudanese women with bare breasts and shaved heads, and Tuareg women with uncovered heads.

The slave women were displayed in scanty clothing—just like that Andalusian woman, dazzlingly white, like a night lit up by a full moon, with an indolent expression in her eyes and that camelia tint in her complexion which intense heat imparts to feminine flesh. She wore only a light, sleeveless tunic, open in front, showing her firm breasts, her flat stomach and narrow waist. Her wavy blond hair hung down to her behind. Her waist was as dainty as a leather cord and her full legs were as smooth as papyrus stems. The necklace around her long plump neck reflected the sun's rays. The tip of her proud nose, perfectly sculpted, was covered in a sheen of sweat.

The Sudanese slave women were completely naked except for their genitals, which were covered by strings of precious carnelian pearls or shells hanging down from a belt, highlighting the steatopygia of these black Callipygian Venuses, some of whose hips were swaying to the marvelous sounds of a wooden flute played by a magician eunuch. Some sang along to the flute in a murmur made charming by their slight accent and soft pronunciation.

The crowd's eyes feasted on the delicate lips, the small mouths, the white teeth, the fresh cheeks, the steady eyelids, the smooth hair, the perfect waists, the soft busts, the beauty and perfection of the facial features, the eyes, the even noses, the whiteness of the teeth and the brilliance of the skin. A few visitors stuck out their heads with flared nostrils to savor the troubling pleasure of feminine odors. A Barbar eunuch, as plump as the Buddha, was showing off the merchandise.

"Come one, come all! See how beautiful they are! They are all of noble origin. Look at this one, for example," he said, placing his hand on the narrow waist of one of the slave women. "You can have her for only two hundred and fifty dinars. Come closer! Come closer! You can even touch them!"

That's when I saw al-Nacrani come crawling along like an insect, sticking his head out, letting his hooked nose wander from one slave to the next.

Across from the slave stall was the weapons stall, with lances of every length, bows and arrows, sharp-edged sabers glinting in the sunlight, and *lamt* shields piled up in tall stacks. To the right of the slave stall was the Word stall, where orators lined up to sell words by the kilo: poetry, prose, panegyric, satire, love, wisdom, rhetoric, madness... Dreams and wonders from distant lands. A babbling and avid crowd pressed up to the front of the stall: poets searching for an unobtainable rhyme, misers looking to mend old harps from their folly, foreign minds searching for new words to replace their words as worn out as the soles of wind, and who sometimes ran across never-before spoken words that sounded like the cries of a newborn; self-important men searching for a cheap and easy accolade, nostalgic men rummaging through the leftover words... One man was rummaging with both hands, under tongues and in every corner of mouths, searching, he said, for the last syllable he needed to assemble the Word, the one in which all words would come to be resolved. And, going from orator to orator, a veiled woman, in magnificent clothing revealing only her large eyes full of unfathomable sadness, gathered words from the very mouths of the orators into an enormous horn that she occasionally slipped under her veils at mouth-level...

There was also this short and very ugly man with a large head who came every day to buy new words that he laid out before us in a composition that was new every time, but that always said the same thing. He addressed the slaves in their language and tried to converse with them. It seemed to me that he paid particularly close attention to me.

"You are human beings like the others, like those who claim to be your masters. You are even superior to them, for sin has debased them. Evil debases man. Free yourselves!"

People didn't seem to hear his tirade, but the slave merchants and a few other men around the stall shot him perfidious glances.

In the evenings, when the milling crowd left, when its clamor dissipated into the sky along with the dust from their feet, the slaves would light a big fire and sing lengthy lamentations, haunting and sad, to the sound of the *gneibra*, a small, single-stringed lute that a certain Matalla played with a thumb pick. The man with the large head would join us, take pleasure in the singing and the music, and, between songs, exhort us to revolt. I remained on display for weeks without anyone wanting to buy me. Then one day, a certain Z'baqra took me in exchange for a few dinars.

My new owner's house was located near the great mosque of Awdaghost, in a narrow and silent street threaded between massive, austere houses with very few entrances. When I arrived there for the first time, the faithful were leaving the mosque after the afternoon prayer. The main entrance to the street opened out between two brick benches lining the wall. The carefully decorated threshold containing a staircase gave the entrance to the abode an imposing appearance. The entrance had one sturdy door made up of three wooden panels, trimmed with large nails rimmed in metal. A hefty ring of hammered copper served as a door-knocker. The entrance opened up onto a vestibule that sheltered a brick bench for the doorman. A massive epigraphed plaque was suspended above the door of the foyer, which was very spacious. Its walls were carefully covered in delicate Banco and a spotless tiled floor. The northwest corner was taken up by the first steps of a staircase that led up to the terrace. The foyer connected to another room by a raised threshold and to the courtyard by another, smaller threshold. The extensive courtyard held a dozen little stick huts with domestic servants running around between them.

I heard music and a soft voice singing wistfully. A young woman was sitting in the shade, upon a lattice cot, in front of the doorway to the corridor. She was surrounded by men eyeing her hungrily and was playing pleasant notes on a harp. Her long flowing hair was adorned with little jewels in gold filigree, leather pouches, and amulets. Her bare chest was decorated by a wide necklace with a trefoil-shaped pendant also in gold filigree; she wore silver bracelets trimmed with beads of the same metal. The men were trying to outdo each other by improvising verses to accompany her melody.

Z'baqra turned me over to a one-eyed man who looked like a galley slave captain. He motioned to me, and I followed him across a vestibule that served as a passageway between the residential courtyard and the service courtyard, located in the back. Back there were the latrines and an open-air kitchen where servants covered in sweat were bustling around the steaming pots resting on traditional hearthstones. The galley slave captain left me in the kitchen. He came back almost immediately with a huge bundle of dirty laundry that he threw at me, pointing at the ashes and buckets in the corner of the kitchen.

"Wash that! And I mean clean! If it's not, I'll make you do it again and beat you the second time around! Go on! Faster!" he barked, prodding me with his foot on my back.

"And where do I go to get water?" I asked him in a piti-ful voice that caused a few other servants to raise their eyes.

"At the well in the other courtyard!"

And he left me, arms limp at my sides, shoulders slumped, not knowing where to start. When I took the buck-ets to go draw the water in the residential courtyard, a resi-due of curiosity made me glance toward the beautiful wom-an on the lattice cot. She was still there, surrounded by her suitors. She had put down her harp and was holding a few heads upon her lap, playing with their hair and murmuring something that was making her smile.

I went back to the kitchen with the buckets full of wa-ter splashing against my legs, and I began to wash the laun-dry with the ashes. A young slave girl was grinding seeds in a mortar. She was standing, a sleeping child straddling her back, and held in both hands a long pestle that she lifted up and pounded down into the bottom of the mortar. Each of her movements was accompanied by a hoarse cry that came from the depths of her being, expressing pain and inevitability. Two old slaves with flat, limp breasts hanging to their knees were arguing violently, each one poking her fingers into the eyes and nostrils of the other. Their kinky white hair, balding in long wide furrows, reflected the sunlight along with the drops of sweat beaded on their temples and foreheads.

When night fell, the galley slave captain, who was happy with the laundry so spared me a beating, led me from room to room, showing me how to light the oil lamps and how to maintain the little hearths at the entrances of the living quarters where incense burned to drive off the mosquitoes. In the morning, he called for me and sent me to the marketplace:

"Here's thirty-five dinars. The master is having a friend over for dinner tonight. Go to the marketplace to buy us a nice, plump dog and five liters of good millet beer!"

"A dog! But I don't know how to tell the difference between a plump dog and a scrawny dog!"

"Oh well, then go back to the kitchen! You'll never amount to anything!"

When the call to prayer rang out throughout the house, the master called me to accompany him to the mosque. I was to follow him, carrying his prayer rug and ablution kettle. Constructed of stone blocks plastered with red earth, like the houses in the city, the mosque formed quite the campus. The buildings were located in the middle of a courtyard whose outer walls were also made of stones covered in mortar. The wide and deep oratory was flanked with two perpendicular wings framing an inner courtyard closed off to the west by the outer wall of the mosque, which had a wide brick bench. This inner courtyard also contained wells and large earthenware jars of water for ablutions. An open-air mihrab was carved into the eastern wall of the oratory. The wings of the mosque controlled access to the inner courtyard. Surrounding the buildings to the north, east, and south, the outer courtyard had three entrances: one in the southwest corner, one in the south wall, and one in the northwest corner. This courtyard was lower than the surrounding streets. We had to go down seven steps to enter it from the west.

Z'baqra sat down in the sun, near the jars of water, to perform the ritual ablution. He washed his hands meticulously, rinsed out his mouth, then his nose, washed his face and forearms three times; rubbed his moistened hands across his head three times, washed his ears and feet, the right foot first and then the left foot. Eyes closed, he moved his lips in inaudible prayer, both hands clasped in front of his face. He stayed this way for a long time, his head bowed, his body bent forward, as if he were breathing in the humidity released from the wet sand under his feet. Then he stood up, took a few steps forward and, standing in front of his shadow, feet together, stood still for a moment, staring at the short, black trail that went from his feet toward the east. He began to measure his shadow: a first step with his right foot, placing the heel directly in front of and touching the top of his left foot, a second step with his left foot and so on. Four steps, the shadow measured four feet: it was time for the first afternoon prayer. He headed toward the minaret, located in the southwest part of the courtyard and climbed up the stairs to reach the top which was crowned with double corbels and four corner merlons. This quadrangular tower rested on a massive socle that was one story high. The entrance to the minaret and the entrance to its stairway were situated on the south side, at the same level as the terrace of the southwest wing. The stairway came out onto a top balcony, forming a sort of pyramid truncated by three degrees and whose doorway opened to the south like that of the minaret itself.

He paused only to regain his breath and then sang out, in a leggero tenor voice, the call to prayer: *"Allahou akbar! Allahou akbar!"* which floated across the labyrinth of narrow streets in the old city immobilized by the Saharan sun. The faithful converged toward the mosque, drawn by the call of the muezzin. Soon, a multicolored crowd filled the oratory. They lined up behind the imam in compact rows parallel to the *qibla* wall.

The oratory was wide and shallow, with only four transverse naves parallel to the *qibla* wall. The quadrangular pillars, with no base or capital, held up high, narrow horseshoe arches with wooden frameworks. The mihrab and the minbar were merged together inside a double rectangular alcove, protruding out of the outer wall. Another mihrab also jutted out. This oratory had seven doors: one in the south wall, four in the west wall, three of which led to the wings and one to the main courtyard; two open doorways were in the east wall, one between the two mihrabs leading directly to the main courtyard, while the other led to the portico. The northwest wing had a door to the main courtyard and three bay windows into the inner courtyard to the south. Two large brick pillars occupied the median of the room. The southwest wing had one doorway to the main courtyard and two doorways to the inner courtyard- vaulted doorways with low horseshoe arches above. This wing had two naves; between the pillars were wide, low archways made of stones placed in a fan shape, with no keystones. Peaceful and austere, no paintings or relief decor adorned the mosque.

The Slave Rebellion

A few years later, Z'baqra founded a school in the mosque. I remained
at his side every day, as long as the lessons lasted, shaking
out his rug, shackling the little children by their feet until
they memorized their Quran, bringing hot coals to keep
warm when it was cold out, organizing the books, bringing
water for ablutions, or massaging the master between lessons
when he was tired. By dint of hearing his lessons, I learned
the Quran, the commentaries, the Arabic language and its
grammar. Then, in time, Z'baqra's school became an Ibadi
center renowned throughout Africa and even all the way to
Andalusia. I never missed a single one of the frequent jousts
between the students regarding questions such as ability and
accident and their relationship to action, human actions and
their relationship to divine creation, the annihilation of the
universe, minor infidelity and major infidelity, the status of
the children of *shirks* who associate other deities with God,
the status of hypocrites; the question of proof and prophecy,
that of revelation and miracles, etc. All these questions no
longer held any secrets for me.

One day, I tossed my bucket down into the well and was surprised by the sharp noise it made at the bottom upon hitting nothing. I leaned over to look: the bucket was resting on a big rock and the well was dry. I ran to alert my one-eyed boss.

"What? How can it be dry? If you're lying, I'm gonna kill you!" And he went to lean his own head into the well.

"There is no longer a single drop of water! Even yesterday it was still bursting with water! What a disaster! Take the buckets and go to the mosque to get some water."

But out of the three wells at the mosque, two had also completely dried up. The other one, much deeper, still held a bit of water. I took a double length of rope, tied the ends together to be able to reach the bottom, and, by scraping around a lot, I was able to pull up one bucketful. At afternoon prayer, the rumor was on everyone's lips: "The wells are dry!" After prayer, the men remained in place, petrified by this event. The imam stood up and said:

"I call you all to come early tomorrow morning to the gates of the city, on the al-Beidha hill; we will say the prayer of *istisqa*."

The next day, the men donned their great white robes trimmed in red and their turbans and headed out toward the city gate. They walked slowly, stooping over, murmuring prayers of pardon. They had all draped the ends of their turbans on their right shoulders. They gathered at the top of the white hill and lined up in compact rows behind the imam. After two prostrations, as is done during Eid prayers, the imam stood up and faced the faithful, lecturing them about their sins, inviting them to return to the path of righteousness, and imploring God's pardon. Then, he turned his back to them again, moving the end of his turban from his right shoulder to his left shoulder. The faithful, who remained seated, imitated him by each moving his turban to his left shoulder. Then the short man with the large head stood up:

"I also invite you to return to reason, even if it is now too late. This town is a purgatory long since given over to anarchy and corruption. Your immoderation and your arrogance will bring about your downfall. You see nothing in this city but a paradise for trading gold and slaves. You have built giant furnaces for melting gold and copper, and for making glass and leaded brass which have turned the sustaining water table, as well as all the nearby woods, into steam and smoke. You have over-consumed both water and wood, for several centuries and out of all proportion with the real possibilities of water accumulation, let alone the reproduction of trees. You are the ones who are responsible for depleting the water table, drying up the wells, and degrading the vegetation base, all of which will soon make life impossible in this city. The Sanhajas are right to want to redraw the trans-Saharan trade routes to avoid Awdaghost, for you have turned this city into a parasitic organism with excessive demands, which has disrupted the equilibrium of this region. Yes, they are right to want to change things, these

51

followers of Ibn Yasin who make you tremble in fear because they will put an end to your life of debauchery, destroy your musical instruments, and prohibit your fermented drinks and your dog-meat roasts! You pay no attention to the affairs of this world, except for food and women. Outside of that, nothing is worth your attention. Now, go, return to your houses, make your slaves dig even deeper wells, you might find some water, but it will only put things off temporarily. You might manage to survive a few more decades, but this madness will come to an end and the day will come when all traces of its memory will be lost."

During this dark time, I met Vala, a beautiful Berber slave who would also come to scrape the bottom of the mosque wells. This wholesome girl had light eyes, like a luminous sky cleansed by a storm. I went to meet up with her every evening, in an abandoned house in the craft district, on a narrow street where the rumors of the city were muted. Late into the night, as the mountain whistled in the wind, and as the cold cracked open the rocks, we would light little fires in the bygone hearths. Then strange shadows would begin to appear on the walls and the house would once again be filled with the ghosts of its past.

The wind would carry to us snippets of noises snatched from the city, an isolated cry, a lost syllable, a disembodied musical note or a call to prayer that would be lost as they made contact with the residual echoes. Sometimes, we would roam the sidewalk-less streets of the neighborhood, savoring the balmy night air. When we wanted to see each other during the day, I would meet her in a cave halfway up the cliff. The entrance was hidden by a huge pile of fallen rocks where hyraxes and rock pigeons made their dwellings. We would sometimes stay there until nightfall. From this observation post overlooking the city, she liked to watch the ships of the desert depart in long unhurried convoys. I hated this sight and instead watched her well-proportioned profile, her unkempt brown hair, her wrinkled gauze tunic, and the fleeting expressions that brought color to her dreamy face.

One day, she asked me to come earlier. And when, after the first prayer of the afternoon, my one-eyed boss sent me to get water, I left the buckets next to the well and hurried to meet up with her. I climbed the pile of rocks fallen from the cliff, which was steep at that spot, and arrived in the cave covered in sweat and out of breath. She was there, her face calm, radiant in the cool shadow. When I caught my breath, she began to speak to me gently. She revealed to me that for some time now, she had been taking an active part in preparing for the slave rebellion.

"Just think! There are dozens of us in each house here; some of the wealthy traders each have more than a thousand slaves. We can take the city and run them off, even more easily now that many of the wealthy plan to flee toward Ghana, ahead of the al-Murabitun invasion. Ibn Yasin and his Sanhajas have already seized Sijilmasa and the caravans returning from there speak of an imminent attack on Awdaghost. We need you. Apparently, you have become a scholar of theology. We need your help to get religion on our side. We won't see each other again tonight; you'll go meet up with Matalla in the craft district; he'll be there after the *Isha* prayer."

Before leaving, she took me by the hand and told me, as natural as can be, as if it were unlikely to have any repercussions: "Soon, there will be three of us. I'm pregnant with your baby. If it's a boy, we will name him Matalla."

Since I found no words to answer her, she added, "Don't forget about the meeting tonight."

She left the cave and slowly started down the rock pile, like a perfectly tranquil gazelle.

That evening, I dreamed of future me.

I was a thousand years old, chained up in the back of a truck taking me toward an unknown destination. The route went through low ocher-colored buildings stacked up along the slope of a cliff, between jumbled piles of large stone blocks. The structures were flooded by yellow light disseminated by powerful projectors. The truck went through a circular intersection. A huge portrait took center stage on a billboard right in the middle. The dark face exuded ferocity. The whites of the eyes embedded behind overly prominent eyebrows were brilliant. The flat nose with enormous nostrils was turned up, preventing the thick lips from touching each other, making his expression stuck in a perpetual hideous smile. Below the portrait was the inscription: "His Excellency Tangalla Ould Matalla, President of the Democratic Republic of Barzakh."

The first night, Matalla gathered us in a square courtyard lit up by the moon. There were about twenty of us. He opened the discussion by saying that we had to find a religious justification for the rebellion, and for that they had to know if Islam permitted slavery and under what conditions, and if a Muslim had the right to keep another Muslim in slavery.

"We must also determine the moment when the rebellion becomes justified and if, during a legal revolt, we have the right to kill a Muslim enemy."

Several participants expressed conflicting views on all these questions, putting forth arguments drawn from the Quran and from the tradition of the Prophet and his companions.

"We must first prepare materially for the revolt before seeking its moral justification. We haven't even found weapons yet. If the rebellion starts now, it will be crushed and drenched in blood."

"So, then we do not have the right to revolt! It would be a suicide and a sin. Didn't the Prophet say, 'He among you who observes a wrong must right it by his own hand if he can, either by his words or in his own conscience...'?"

"But you forget that he added, 'And that is the lowest level of faith'!"

"Why all this judicial-theological nitpicking? We are slaves and natural reason justifies our rebellion. In this purgatory, this barzakh, there are limits to freedom and laws that allow men to be treated like things and not like people!

Yet, it's an absolute principle that no actual constraint can be exerted against man, for each man is a free essence, capable of asserting his free will in the face of necessity and of rejecting everything that belongs to his present reality. This is how constraint and revolt are related!"

"That's enough! Stop this infidel!"

"Idolater!"

"Filth!"

"Low-life *shirk*!"

"*Dahriste*!"

"Stop it! Don't talk all at once, one at a time. And respect the others' points of view. You there, you no longer have the right to speak! Let the others speak—you can speak another time. You over there, speak!"

"First, I want us to define who are our enemies and our friends. For example, look at the rich slaves who do not pay their *zakat*—can we consider them friends? And those who sell female slaves before abstaining for one menstrual period in observance of the *Istibrā*'? And the children of our masters, should we view them as friends or as enemies?"

"As for the children of our masters, Thaalaba has already provided the answer: they cannot be viewed as friends or as enemies. We must wait until they come of age and have been called to Justice—if they embrace it, they are friends, if they reject it, they are enemies! As for the conditions for selling female slaves, the religious prescriptions are clear: he who sells a female slave and delivers her to the buyer before she has had her period is one of those sinful men who destroy the bonds that God has imposed and who corrupts the Earth. It is the emir's duty to drive off those guilty of such a practice by enforcing punishment by exile. The emir should not believe someone who claims he hasn't slept with his slave unless it concerns an unattractive girl. The practice of *Istibrā'* is mandatory for concubine slaves as well as for any slave with whom the master has slept with following his declaration or with established proof, even if it concerns an unattractive girl. He is required to leave the slave with a trustworthy man until she has menstruated!"

"For me, anyone who trades slaves—male or female—is an enemy, whether he observes the legal prescriptions or not. I repeat to you once again: it comes down to an issue of natural rights. For us to make our case and be recognized as free, we must reject the present reality. Since men must come into conflict with each other, by striving to express themselves and assert themselves, those who have chosen life over freedom turn out to be powerless to act for themselves, incapable of handling their own independence, and thereby entering into servitude. We are here tonight because we have decided to rebel, to die for our freedom. We have chosen freedom over life!"

"Oh, my God, be my witness that I reject the words of this infidel!"

"Yes, we reject what this atheist has to say!"

"Better to die in servitude and faith than live in freedom and disbelief!"

It was just before dawn when Matalla postponed the debates

to continue them the next evening at the same place. After that, we met up every night, for almost a month, without gaining any ground. We were now divided into several factions, each one with its leader. There were those who thought that the rebellion was not yet justified, that we must first try to reason with the masters; those who thought that we could rebel as long as we strictly followed the legal prescriptions; those who felt we must first identify enemies and friends. There were also those who supported legal slavery and those in favor of death for freedom. I admitted my disappointment to Vala:

"These slaves are too divided; they'll never manage to pull anything off!"

But her optimism remained unshaken.

"We will succeed, you'll see! Be patient for another few nights and a mutual solution will be found, I'm sure of it!"

Then, she suggested that we go see her grandmother.

"You'll see, she's amazing. She speaks like an oracle. She'll tell you about your future!"

We found her grandmother sitting in the corner of a courtyard, in front of a little hut made of worn-out burlap. Vala took my left hand and held it up to her eyes.

"Grandmother, this is Gara, my friend. You're going to give him tidings from his future."

The old woman lifted her wrinkled forehead to me, lowered her head to look at my palm, and immediately pushed it away in fear, turning her back to me. Vala was worried.

"Grandmother! Grandmother! What's wrong? Why don't you want to read my friend's palm?"

The grandmother answered with a wave of her hand, as if she wanted us to leave her alone. But Vala refused to give up. She pestered so much that the old lady ended up murmuring:

"I think, my daughter, that the gods have fallen on their heads or have grown tired of my questions and are now trying to drive me crazy!"

"But Grandmother, you didn't even take the time to look at his hand!"

"I didn't need time, everything appeared to me in an instant!"

"And?"

"It's so strange! I've never seen such a life line! It's monstrous!"

"Grandmother!"

"No, be quiet! Since you keep insisting, the oracle will speak: the city is entirely full of both incense smoke and muezzin calls mixed with laments! This man will drink at the wellspring of eternity, but he will be killed by his descendant!"

"Your grandmother's crazy!" I said to Vala, holding my index finger to my temple and making a half-circle motion with it.

"Go ahead, Gara, make fun of me and insult my oracles! But no man before you will ever have been so crushed by destiny! You can never with a clear mind judge the past by the future!"

"Grandmother! Grandmother! What does that mean?"

"There is nothing more to add, my daughter. The oracle has spoken!"

One night, tired of the interminable discussions, Matalla decided to move things along and had us vote on the different options. Those in favor of strictly following the legal prescriptions won by a few votes. The minority factions accused Matalla of having abused his power.

"It's not fair! You should have given the other points of view enough time to make their case, to convince more people."

The night was moonless and we had lit a big fire to give us some light. We were working on the manifesto based on the approach that had won the vote, when suddenly we heard fearsome shouts and men armed with hefty clubs were upon us, coming from all directions. In the firelight, I glimpsed Z'baqra's one-eyed slave, with a reptilian expression on his face, then felt a stunning blow on the back of my neck that make me cry out in a strangled voice and see thousands of stars, and then everything collapsed, myself included.

When I awoke, I was dripping with putrid filth and floundering in a foul morass of sticky muck: I was trapped in the bottom of a latrine cesspit. From time to time, someone would throw some leftovers down to me, or give me a drink with water that had been used to wash dishes or laundry.

One day, I felt something move on my right shoulder. I put my hand on it. It was a rope, and I heard the one-eyed man's voice order me to climb up. I tied the slack rope around my waist and held on with my numb hands. He pulled me out of the pit and threw me into a corner of the kitchen. I stayed there for several days, my head in the ashes, unable to move. The slaves gave me food and drink, without ever speaking a word to me.

The only human being who spoke to me during those days of suffering was the short man with the large head. I was lying in the open-air kitchen with one of the now-cold hearth stones under my head as a pillow, gazing with wide-open eyes at the full moon, unable to sleep, calling out to fate: *Why evil? Why divide men into masters and slaves? How could my father, who begot, raised, and protected me, abandon me to slavery?* These questions were assailing my mind like bats when I heard the voice of the short man with the large head.

"In bygone days," he said, "Good reigned supreme in the world, but became bored. One day, he began doubting himself and imagined that there was another who was his opposite. And Evil was born. Ever since, he ceaselessly expands his kingdom, exiling Good further and further away each day."

"And men?" I interrupted.

"Men? They are the latest invention of Evil, his most formidable ruse. Look, for example, at the one who denounced you."

"We were denounced?"

"You were denounced by one of the slaves who was in the minority."

"I give up on understanding any of it! I no longer seek anything but this: to escape from my servitude and live in another era where men are better!"

"Perhaps you will manage to do that one day. If you contest your fate, flee from men and go into the desert!"

I had looked away from the sky and was now staring at the short man who was speaking to me: *How ugly!* I thought. *Repulsively ugly. Yet, through the expression of his mouth and from the look in his eyes, there is a hint of an immeasurably beautiful being animating this grotesque mask.*

The Cosmic Dimension

I remained in the kitchen until the day when, tied to the tail of a camel, I left Awdaghost with the caravan to Sijilmasa. By dawn, the white ridge of Awdaghost had already disappeared over the horizon toward the south. The caravan had reached its cruising speed and was crossing a wooded region full of gum trees, following a long continuous corridor between towering swells of sand dunes. I discovered a new pleasure when I felt my bare feet sink into the still-fresh sand to the rhythm of my steps. But very soon, I began to feel the painful efficiency of its abrasive properties. After the first hour of trekking, walking became an increasingly atrocious torture. Luckily, the camel that pulled me kept bucking and throwing off its load, which made for frequent stops.

Each stage was followed by another, with the same endless monotony: we loaded up the camels at the break of day, walked until the sun was directly over our heads, at the hottest point when the light erased our shadows. Then we unloaded the beasts and hobbled them; we unpacked the sacks that contained the food, the supplies to make a fire, and the tools for repairing the goatskins and sacks; we put up shelters to create a bit of shade and to protect ourselves from the heat and wind. Then we all became motionless in the ambient immobility, like a malignant gall on the surface of this quartz universe. And when the sun relented, we started off again and walked for the rest of the day and kept going for the first third of the night. Then we halted wherever we happened to be and spent the rest of the night there until dawn. Then the next stage would begin.

The almost permanent view of the sky above my head had caused me to expand. As a result of seeing so many stars, I had acquired a cosmic dimension and I saw the sand as dust from stars that had run aground on Earth. As the caravan relentlessly advanced along its route, the quartz appeared in all its facets across the immensity of sand—hard, black, red, white, spread out or in layers, piled up in crumbling dunes topped with ever-shifting ridges.

After several days of walking, the caravan came along-side an imposing wall of rocks, from ocher to purplish-black in color, that we crossed at a point where the escarpment disappeared entirely under the swells of sand. The animals formed a single file line, nose to tail, with the slaves attached to the camels, walking off to the side. The men of the car-avan walked in front, behind, and alongside the long line, keeping an eye on how well the loads were balanced and tied down, leading the convoy. The soft sand of the cres-cent dunes engulfed the hoofs of the heavily loaded beasts.

The pass led to a rocky area on the other side that stretched out for several kilometers before giving way to lower, simpler sand formations, with the occasional rocky outcropping sticking up. Then began a vast peneplain with thin rows of linear dunes rising up here and there. It was striking how consistently fine-grained the sand was and how varied and contrasting its colors were.

Our shadows swiftly caught up to us, wiped out by the sun. It was time for our halt. The harmattan wind whipped our faces, burned our eyes, and chapped our lips. We put up shelters to create a bit of shade and protect ourselves from the heat and the wind. The slaves prepared tea, watching over the camels or massaging their masters as they stretched out on the sand. One merchant, who had fallen from a camel during the trip, was lying on his back in the sun and was having his slave bury him in the hot sand to ease the soreness of his muscles and bones.

One time, the caravan halted to let the animals benefit from a good pasture of *atil*, or Maerua crassifolia Forssk, that might not be found up ahead. This bush, with its tightly interwoven branches that can sometimes cause injury, provides rich fodder that is excellent for camels. One drop of rain! The weather was very oppressive, indicating a storm. The sun disappeared behind a dark gray wall sprinkled with red and black spots; the storm raged, but in the sky at very high altitudes, and the rain evaporated before it hit the ground; only a few miraculous drops made it all the way down to the hot sand. The atmosphere, saturated with electricity, disoriented the camels. We hurried to depart, hoping to get out of the phantom storm's reach.

Another day, the caravan halted in a deep basin surrounded by very high white linear dunes with an occasional shifting erg rising even higher. Horse antelopes, busy grazing, raised their heads and ran off as the caravan approached. Sparsely scattered myrrh trees grew down here, with their knotted, dangerous-looking branches, resembling miniature bao-babs with more slender trunks; and umbrella thorn acacias that looked remarkably like their namesake with multiple, gnarled trunks holding up branches that curved down in all directions and were covered with bluish-green leaves grow-ing in an alternating pattern. There were also a few Sodom apple trees—so-called testicle trees, with large opposing leaves and bunches of flowers clustered together in a corymb structure that provided abundant latex—an indication of an ancient human presence buried beneath the sand. Crawling along the base of the trees were the colocynths with their long offshoots heavily laden with fruit. Ligneous vines were climbing up the trunks, some of which had fallen and were crawling along the ground, interwoven with the branches of the colocynths. All around, the sand remained immaculate, as devoid of vegetation as the spotless blue sky that reflected in the eyes of the camel drivers.

The shackles were removed from the slaves. The risk of an escape attempt decreased with every step the caravan took into the Great Desert, a land with no landmarks and no water, a land of lost souls and those who die of thirst. I had remained in the sun, thrusting my arms into the sand to seal up the open wounds left by the rope. The motionless heat had woven its web of light, immobilizing all beings within their minuscule shadows. The camels knelt in their own shadows, facing the sun, following the immemorial instinct of their species.

How did this universe, which has witnessed the birth of so many creatures, lose everything to preserve only these few men and their animals? It's not possible that these unjust and corrupt men could be better than all the creatures they have outlived. How could God have willed it to be this way?

No matter how much I twisted and turned my arms in the incandescent quartz sand, closing my eyes and letting my spirit bathe in the viscous purple universe of the formless substance, I could not find a justification for the persistence of humanity.

These dunes of immaculate white sand, bathed in light, would be infinitely true and beautiful if it weren't for the pollution of human beings.

The call to prayer echoed between the dunes. The men anointed their faces and hands with sand and then, turning toward the east, lined up behind one of them whose words they repeated and whose movements they imitated. I joined them with a profound sense of the absurd: Why this equality in prayer and not in life? Why adhere to the formal precepts of religion and ignore its foundations by living in evil and injustice?

We brought back the camels and led them through the long corridor formed by the two rows of half-loads that had already been lined up; then we had them kneel in front of the corresponding load. The packsaddles were put on and loaded up amid the bustling and shouting of men and beasts. Then we had these ships of the desert stand up one by one and the caravan started off again. The animals formed a single file with the men scurrying all around them, like a swarm of bees. The slaves, who were now walking with hands untied for the first time, seemed happy. As for me, I still felt just as hopeless. It wasn't the physical pain that I felt the most, in spite of the still-bleeding wounds on my wrists, and despite the abrasive sand that scoured the skin off the soles of my feet. I suffered from the pain of being man, of belonging to the human species.

The sun was already upon its throne above the highest dunes, but the wind had not yet picked up; the barkhan dunes had barely started to smoke as the wind blew a thin swirl of quartz from the tops of their slopes. Long, mysterious shadows fled toward the west, hugging the curves of the sand. The caravan reached a huge massif of disordered dunes that, driven by the eastern wind, were slowly crumbling away down the full length of their western face, a raging sea of sand whose shifting dunes, under constant pressure to attack one another, formed an enormous ocean wave frozen at the very moment it begins to break. This extremely difficult terrain made walking particularly slow and painful for the men, but even more so for the beasts that struggled to move forward under the weight of their loads. The branches of a foundering acacia tree emerged out of the shifting dunes like clenched hands. There were many dama gazelles in this region. The slaves got a few in the hunt for the evening meal. They also caught some fawns who bleated dreadfully in the middle of the loads, up on the backs of the camels.

The sun was setting rapidly, delivering to the night the eastern faces of the dunes, over which it was already spreading its cloak of darkness that would soon cover the entire earth. The shadows faded away slowly, suffocated by the swell of sand. The sun had removed its garment of light and its nudity was the same color as the quartz that the night had not yet won over. It was at this moment that, up on the horizon, two N'madis and their pack of Sloughi dogs appeared in profile, as unreal as their evanescent shadows. In a single motion, they began to race down and back up the crumbling jumble of slopes all the way to the caravan, stirring up the sand along the way, in a series of landslides. The men were naked as newborns, even more naked than their dogs. They were overcome with fatigue and thirst. One of the men of the caravan hurried to catch up to a camel that carried a goatskin flask; he unhooked a large wooden bowl, called a slave to untie the string that held the goatskin shut, and collected the water in the bowl. When it was full, he brought it to the N'madis who dunked their heads into it at the same time as their dogs did, drinking as much as they could. The arrival of the nomadic hunters did not disturb the rhythm of the caravan's laborious march up the slopes and back down into low areas, across the increasingly loose sand.

"Eeeeeeha! Eeeeeeha!" the slaves continued to sing out in unison to spur on the loaded pack camels.

Waves with steep slopes, often crescent-shaped along the top, presented a disorderly chaos with features that sometimes took on paroxysmal proportions, forcing the caravan to make long detours in search of calmer areas with more subdued formations.

We halted during the first third of the night and lit a big fire to roast the gazelles. The play of shadow and light transformed faces into terrifying masks. The men devouring the grilled meat took on the appearance of ferocious beasts. All around, darkness had hidden the earth, showing the firmament in all its radiance. Invisible presences prowled around the camp: white ants, beetles, lizards, jerboas, phantoms, and, always on the lookout, the inevitable fennec fox of the Saharan sand, omnipresent, resourceful robber of meat, filled with nocturnal audacity.

The camp gave itself over to the gentleness of the night. An infinity of stars—bright or faint, nearby or faraway—studded the celestial vault. The Milky Way unfurled its immense carpet of light across the sky. Suddenly the N'madis' dogs, wrested from their lethargy, pricked up their ears and, raising their heads to the sky, started to howl strangely. And just then, coming from the east, there appeared in the firmament an enormous comet with blurry edges whose blinding light grew brighter as it rose in the sky, its long crystalline braids flowing behind. There were no other stars in the sky as the earth was lit up by a thousand suns. Then the comet fell toward the west and its light gradually faded away. Night came back to the earth and the firmament regained its brilliance. Immobilized by the vast silvery trail, the camp remained silent; a nameless fear had gripped men and beasts alike. Their faces were horrified, their eyes bulged, their mouths and panting jaws hung open. The men of the caravan saw the comet's apparition as a sign of divine vengeance and an omen of the impending end of the world.

"It's a miracle bringing a message to decipher!"

"There will be a decade of great suffering!"

"The end of the world will happen this year!"

With the apparition of the comet, I felt like I was breaking free of gravity; I became lighter. I felt myself get bigger. My perception became multidimensional. The comet had changed my state, but my physical and mental wounds persisted. In fact, I felt them more intensely. I stayed awake all night, a wild look in my eyes, my mind drowning in the unfathomable mystery of my destiny. *What an extraordinary change! I glided over the sand as if I was walking on water! The soles of my feet barely skimmed the surface of the still-frozen quartz!* The camels couldn't get over it. As for the men, they were blinded by their stubbornness. At dawn, my master bluntly reminded me of the reality of my condition. I lit the fire and helped put the packsaddles on the beasts and load them up.

The N'madis whistled for their dogs and disappeared into the sand, heading west.

The beasts were already loaded up, ready to be stood up for the departure, and the men of the caravan were checking the tie-downs one last time when a slave, probably driven insane by the comet's passing, leaped at his master's neck and started to strangle him. About ten men, most of them slaves, rushed to the master's aid. They yanked on the deranged slave's arms and beat him soundly. But nothing helped, every ounce of his extraordinary strength manifested in his hands that squeezed harder and harder. The master's face became dangerously pale, and his tongue grew longer and longer as it dangled out of his mouth. Then one of the men of the caravan grabbed a sharp ax and split the skull of the wretched slave who, letting out a horrible cry, collapsed with his hands still clenched around the throat of his master, whom he had taken down with him as he fell. They broke the slave cadaver's fingers one by one to separate him from his victim. His sticky yellow brain slowly poured out onto the blood-soaked sand. The victim's body was washed with his ration of water and his assassin's ration. They wrapped him in a piece of new, white cloth and lined up, placing the body in front of them, faces turned toward the east. After a prayer without prostrations, they proceeded to bury him.

The caravan entered a region distinguished by low-lying formations with a framework of low, moving linear dunes that appeared just as the crumbling crescent dunes disappeared.

Sand accumulated in the thin, tangled branches of the *awarach* bushes that the camels liked so much, stretching out like tongues, often more than two meters long, forming cones with right angles at the top. We knelt the camels in a row to relieve them of their loads, then let them stand up to graze on the providential bushes that would become more and more scarce along the way. The baggage remained in place, as it was, ready to be loaded back up.

The first broom shrubs marked a new botanical frontier. The valleys were scattered with frequent black scabs, each one with a diameter nearly a meter wide. Fear and thirst gradually increased as the caravan forged ahead farther and farther into the Great Desert. Freely quenching thirsts was no longer an option. The water went bad, turned black, and started to stink despite the goatskins being soaked in butter and pitch. Yet this did not stop the men of the caravan from coveting it every night, trying to steal a mouthful from the communal reserves that were strictly rationed. But the chromatic changes to their urine—from pale lemon yellow to dark mahogany and then to the color of port wine— unmasked those who had secretly drank some during the night, so they could be punished by depriving them of their ration during the day.

The last dunes had strikingly gentle shapes and arresting feminine curves. Their sand, perfectly clean and noble, wept under the feet of the caravan; the play of shadow and light upon their infinite facets lent them a sorrowful and eternal appearance. In calm areas, the low, narrow linear dunes formed the shiny bones of a quartz skeleton polished by the sun and the wind.

To keep warm during the nighttime stopovers, the men of the caravan lit great fires, which they ceased feeding with wood a few hours before dawn. Then they curled up around these extinguished hearths and, in spite of the terrible cold, always fell asleep within moments, out of exhaustion. On one of these dark, cold nights, when the reddish glow from the embers had already faded away under a thick layer of ash, I was suddenly torn from my deep slumber by a strange and unusual embrace. I felt a firm flesh, swollen and moist, against my naked skin, and the tense and panting body of a man against my body. I let out a violent kick to the stomach of this pleasure thief and, in a single bound, was far from the mass of sleeping caravan men. I spent the rest of the night on the lookout, in an impregnable fortress on the top of a dune, far from any source of heat.

The Shepherd's star was still sparkling with all its crystal light when I felt myself being shaken vigorously and heard the rough voice of my master who insulted me and ordered me to get up for the unavoidable morning chores. I ran down the crumbling slope of the dune, barely feeling the still-frozen sand under my feet. I got some wood and lit the fire; thick vapor poured from my mouth and made a cloud in front of my face.

The men of the caravan were prostrated for morning prayer. I tried in vain to recognize the man who had embraced me the night before. Absorbed in prayer, making pious gestures, all the men seemed above suspicion, but I was sure that the sinner was among them. As I went to retrieve the camels, I almost stepped on a sleeping viper. The snake was coiled in the center of a circular area of flat sand, surrounded by a ring of footprints left by small birds.

Before sunrise, the caravan entered a vast region of depressions, dug out by the swirling air and wind, creating many bowls of varying depth that revealed the ground underneath. The most solid parts that had resisted the wind erosion had become table-like mounds. Underneath, arranged in layers with noticeable indentations, was very fine-grained sand, often snowy white, but also sometimes tinged with ash gray, dusty rose, or golden-yellow. In this zone of extremes, the dunes, pushed by very violent winds, swelled up and sank very rapidly into the depths; it was the last phase of their evolution, their fulfillment. Here and there emerged chunks of brown earth or soil covered with a layer of laterite pebbles that had withstood the wind. In the zones of less extreme sand formations, the dunes simply rested on a sort of rocky reg; the highest ones were on the lee side of the depressions that had given them their colors.

The caravan pushed ahead into a small, flat, mirror-like strip where the sand, made up of the fine red grains so characteristic of the region, was nothing but a light veil rippling in the wind. Then began a continuous succession of small, whitish ergs and shifting dunes in uniform, rounded waves like an endless sine wave that transformed the caravan into a sand dragon. Sometimes, the amplitude was almost insignificant, but most of the time it was pronounced enough that it completely blocked the view. Superimposed upon these curves were much larger mounds, almost imperceptible because their slopes were so gentle. But in certain places, they became more discernible, especially in the late hours of the day when the sun, low on the horizon, cast a different light upon them, causing their recurring outlines to stand out.

The trek across these endless undulations was not physically painful—the slopes were very gentle and the sand, constantly smoothed by the wind, remained quite firm underfoot—but it was desolately monotone. Each valley blocked off the surrounding horizon; and never did the eyes encounter the least point of reference. This region was feared by the men of the caravan. In this "land of devils," you had to be strong-minded to keep your bearings, especially when a sandy wind picked up, drowning out everything in sparkling grayscale.

I ended up losing my identity in this universe of red sand devoid of landmarks. Was I the pagan, Gangarian teenager who lived a carefree life in the land of gold of the African savanna, or the Muslim slave who was crossing the expanses of the Great Desert toward an unknown destination, or was I that being haunted by extra-terrestrial elements who had already glimpsed other horizons, or was I all three at the same time?

An idea was becoming more and more clear as it germinated

in my mind: it was no longer a question of going all the way to Sijilmasa. I must escape from my master as soon as I could. But how to leave the caravan without dying of thirst in this fearsome desert? Absorbed in my reflections, I was walking with my head down when I stumbled upon a hillock of halfah grass and disturbed a couple of ratels with identical black and white coats. One of these carnivores leaped at me and it took the intervention of several men armed with sticks to discourage it. The other one attacked the hind legs of a camel: mad with fear, the camel bleated and ran around kicking in every direction to elude it. Men ran to the camel's aid, trying to calm it down: "*Houki! Houki! Kkkk! Kkkk! Karkar! Karkar!*" They attempted to grab it by the neck and by its front legs… Silvery lizards quick as lightning darted in and out of the clumps of grass. These reptiles were baptized "only one more breath," alluding to the immediate effects of their deadly bite.

A fiery wind had started to blow, forcing us to halt in the middle of a stage. The parched men turned on the beasts and killed two camels. They removed their rumens and stuck coils of straw into them, pushing the solid matter to the back walls and gathering the liquid into the little basin thus formed. Then they poked a hole in the center of each rumen and caught its liquid in a bowl. Each of us drank a few mouthfuls of this putrid liquid that saved us all the same. The guide spoke of a well that could be reached tomorrow morning if the caravan walked all night. In any case, the rest of the day was lost: our thirst made it impossible to set off again before sunset. The slaves dug holes, and everyone buried themselves to await the nighttime.

The unrelenting afternoon wore on slowly as if through an hourglass. On the horizon, the long, rounded, fixed dunes broke up a series of elongated, parallel swells. Smaller chains of shifting dunes extended along the summits following the swirling wind on the south slopes— walls of blinding white on a background of reddish sand massifs, each fold as imposing as the next, accentuated by the sheer scope of our perspective, stretching out infinitely toward the west. A herd of addax passed by but no one dreamed of bothering these antelopes as they scratched the ground with their hoofs to dig up the bitter and aqueous *zennoun* roots. Closer to us, a large desert lark picked over a desiccated locust.

In the desert, I had acquired an extraordinary sense of observation, perhaps because of the emptiness, or maybe as a result of the passing comet. I could see every last detail of the least grain of sand. I often watched the twists and turns that took place in the overlooked drama of the infinitely small, which loomed large in my eyes. Like the drama played out by the wasp, its prey, the robber fly, and the camel: the wasp had almost killed its prey, holding it now by the end of its well-sharpened, yellow and white striped stinger. When it felt its prey go completely stiff, it cut off its head, legs, and wings before dragging it off toward its larvae. It was already poised at the entrance to its underground nest when the bloodsucking robber fly landed on its back, thrusting its venomous proboscis into the soft cervical section. It took the wasp in its long black claws, holding it well away from its own body for the brief time it took for paralysis to set in. It was still sucking up the wasp's blood when it felt the impending blow, coming from On High, of an enormous dark mass that quickly blotted out the sky. The robber fly barely had time to lift its triangular forehead, sunken deeply between its eyes, when the apocalyptic mass crushed it and drove it deep into the sand. Predators and prey had just been buried in the same pit, by the random steps of one of the camels of the caravan.

When the fiery red disc, in a gentle descent, sank over the horizon, the men got out of their holes, hastily loaded up the animals, roped them together, and started off on the long nighttime trek. And at the first glimmers of dawn, the guide began to call out, "Ghallawiya! Ghallawiya!" The men of the caravan passed the news from one to another, saying that this was the mountain that had a water source at its base. We spent the day near the well, slaking our thirst, letting the camels drink again and again, refilling the goatskins and washing our tattered garments. Around noon, everything was ready for departure, but the guide wanted to stay the night so the animals could drink one more time in the morning.

That night, the voice of the short man from the Word stall kept tormenting me: "If you contest your fate, flee from men and go into the desert!" I decided to follow his maxim and stayed awake, starry-eyed. A quarter moon faintly lit up the disorderly camp. All around me, faces had taken on the color of slumber. I got up and stealthily slipped between the rows of half-loads, searching for some provisions to take. I happened upon a little burlap sack similar to those that usually held dried meat. I made sure by feeling it before grabbing it along with a good, half-full goatskin and, leaving the sleeping camp behind, I ran toward the mountain, gliding like a fennec fox over the windy, sandy *baten*. In the morning, my footprints—which were pretty shallow to begin with—would be completely erased, deterring any attempt to search for me. And so, without any fear of being disturbed, I could begin my retreat at the top of the mountain.

Part Two

The White Way

Prelude

Black vultures with powerful beaks and long, pink, featherless necks were circling above, on the lookout for carrion. But at regular intervals, I got up and, looking toward the east, raised my arms slightly above my shoulders, and let out a great wail that echoed and reverberated slowly across the mountains: *"Allahu akbar!"* I remained standing, motionless in prolonged expectation, murmuring my prayers. Then, I bent over, head out in front, hands pressed to my knees, with my back and legs making a right angle, then prostrated myself, forehead against the ground, then sat up, then prostrated myself again, sat up again for a moment, and stood up again with the same hoarse cry that got weaker and weaker as the hours passed. I repeated these same movements two times, four times, according to the time of day. At night, jackals prowled around; but each time they got close, my prayers held off the perspective of their feast. A week had already passed since the beginning of my retreat. I fasted during the day, and at night, I drank a bit of water from my goatskin and ate a bit of dried meat. And I prayed.

When I first arrived at the place of my retreat at the top of the mountain, I made the following vow: "I swear never to return to this corrupt humanity and to live away from the unjust, until my death!" My new determination did not seem to have disturbed the order of the world. The sun rose and set as usual; the swirling hot wind, laden with sand, whipped and whistled through the mountains; and the landscape kept that same impassive expression carved into the desert sand and rock by the light and wind. But neither the torrid heat of the day nor the penetrating cold of the night, nor hunger, nor thirst had shaken my firm determination. And any time a flicker of doubt crossed my mind, I heard the voice of the short man saying, "If you contest your fate, flee from men and go into the desert!" Water had run short over the course of the days—I had drunk the last swallow yesterday. Now, each passing hour was torture for my body doomed to hunger and thirst, which abated at night only to make the trial more cruel the following day.

After two days of total fasting, my limbs were stiff and atony had set in, preventing any expression or awareness of prayer. Piety had given way to a profound fear, a dreadful anguish and a ferocious hatred of the human species. Suffering gradually took over my entire body, like quicksand. My lips, mouth, and throat dried out and cracked. My stomach and intestines tightened up and were twisted by a prodigious force, as if it were wringing the last drops of liquid from them. A raging fire burned my entrails, the blaze then spreading up to my face, hands, and chest. When I felt the vultures approach and put their rough feet with sharpened claws upon my body, and strike me with their powerful beaks, my body shook with a violent and desperate convulsion. The vultures let go and leapt back, beating their great outstretched wings.

For hours, atrocious pain radiated through every bone, nerve, and muscle, getting worse in sudden bursts, followed by slow lulls. My head and brain were compressed by a powerful vice, and violent fits of fever racked my body, beginning with severe shivering, then despondency, then gradual euphoria. The pain eased up, the intense spasms stopped, and my legs stretched out. My panting, exhausted flesh no longer needed anything—no longer felt hunger or thirst. I heard buzzing—impressions of chloroform through long sound waves. I felt infinite presences around me, a chorus of friendly voices. The entire desert was full of people watching me die. I was in a new world, where insignificant and bizarre memories of my departing life besieged me like vultures.

A cottony cloud laden with rain had descended from the sky. It rested on my forehead, passed over my face, soaked my lips, passed over my neck, chest, and legs before returning to my forehead. The moisture gradually revived the body and delirium gave way to sensations, but sounds and shapes were still bathed in a blurry haze. The water was now in the entire organism, infiltrating through the pores, irrigating the organs, resuscitating the brain. The proud spirit was reborn from the water.

I was stretched out on my back in the shade of a blurry figure, encircled by a green halo clearly outlined in the air. All around, light flooded the sky and the sun had stretched its immobile coat over the desert. The vultures had disappeared. I was in the same place, at the top of the mountain. Once again, I looked at the blurry figure behind its green halo. I shook with fear and my limbs began to tremble.

"My name is al-Khadir. I am the Green One who guards the sea of time and aids those in distress. You rebel against the human order, but you cannot escape your condition!"

"I would like to live in another era or go back in time, to before my birth, so that I can atone for my great sin of having been born. For in truth, nothing suits me on this earth!"

"I myself go back in time, to alter certain events, prevent certain catastrophes or delay them. Here, for example, I am going to participate in Ibn Yasin's attack on Awdaghost, to destroy the city's furnaces and save the region from an untimely ecological disaster. But such a voyage to the past is impossible for humans because man is incapable of judging the past and the future with a clear head. If you, for example, could go back to the past, you would prevent your parents from meeting each other, but that would be a contradiction since you have already been born! However, what I can offer you is a trip to the future. Of course, you are already taking this trip continually as you naturally get older, but what I propose is much more exciting—it is a passage beyond time. You will be able to stop in one era and stay there if you desire to. But you will also be able to leave it if it does not please you. To do that, you will simply have to retire far away from

85

its inhabitants, as you have just done here. But the new era after this next one will be the last. You will not be able to escape it toward a different future and any return to the past will be impossible. So, you must consider carefully before leaving the next era you will find yourself in. It will be your choice and your responsibility!"

And he faded rapidly away, along with his green halo.

Ghostbuster

I heard approaching voices and footsteps.

"That's strange. It looks like he's asleep!"

"Look, he's breathing! And wearing such odd clothes!"

"To sleep here, in the full sun! In this wind and this heat, at the top of Mount Ghallawiya! He must be a madman!"

"Or back from the dead!"

There were now several of them around me, each one with his own opinion. I could not open my eyes; my heavy eyelids were still soldered shut. I wanted to speak, but no sound came out of my mouth. My fossilized body remained numb, unable to move.

"We must bring him to camp, to show him to Ghostbuster!"

Four of them carried me, each one holding an arm or a leg. When I could squint my eyes open, I saw two black silhouettes filling the sky, dressed in a sort of short, khaki tunic pulled tight at the waist by a wide belt over pleated pants of the same color. They had sand-colored turbans rolled around their necks and guns slung over their shoulders by their straps. I blinked my eyes in the sun. I glimpsed fleeting profiles of prominent cheekbones and flat noses. When I lifted my head a little to get a better look, those holding my legs looked down at me at the same time with red eyes. They descended slowly, walking down a rocky slope that was free of sand.

A camp had been pitched at the edge of the escarpment overlooking the *baten*, at the base of a cliff riddled with cracks. A man with pale white skin was sitting in the shade of a lush caper bush, accompanied by a young woman draped in a loose black veil. Next to them, at the edge of the shade, three men with copper-colored skin bustled around a small fire. They had long black hair and wore large, sleeveless shirts that were open at the neck. There were five in the group who brought me, all of them black. As soon as they saw us, the three lighter-skinned men ran to meet up with us, abandoning the fire that seemed to have been keeping them so busy.

"What's this? Have you found a cadaver?"

"Where did you find him?"

"How has he not been devoured by the vultures and jackals?"

They walked close to me, jostling each other to lean in close to my face or touch me with their hands. They were all speaking at the same time.

"It's not a cadaver; he's still breathing!"

"It looks like he's sleeping!"

"Well, it's a very strange way of sleeping!"

"We found him lying in the full sun, at the top of the mountain!"

"Just a moment ago, he lifted his head and opened his eyes just a bit!"

"Ghostbuster! Ghostbuster! Look what the *tirailleurs* have found!" cried one of the lighter-skinned men walking near my head.

They set me down in the shade, at the feet of the astonished pale man and the draped Venus who had started to cry out, taking cover behind him, as if she had seen a ghost.

"Don't be afraid, my dear, calm down, calm down! It's only a man who was about to die of thirst. That's fine, leave him. What are you all waiting around for? Stoke the fire and hurry up—finish making that tea that's taking forever. And you, go get the camels!"

He took my pulse for a moment and gently laid my arm back down; my heart was beating as regularly as the ticking of a clock in the chamber of a man sentenced to death. He lifted up an eyelid to look into my eye and let it fall again like an iron curtain, but the inside right eyelid muscle slowed its fall and my eye closed gently. Then, pulling on my lower lip, he slipped his index finger into the open space, sliding it across a portion of the left side of my lower jaw, before removing his index finger and letting go of the lip, which snapped back into place like an elastic band, hugging the contours of my mouth. He rubbed his index finger against his thumb, noting a normal amount of salivary secretion. Then he began prodding my entire body, paying close attention to every joint and checking every limb twice. Everything was in place; there was nothing broken. He called over to the men near the fire.

"Mardoucha! Come here; bring me the tea!"

A short, very ugly man with a large head came over with a teapot in his hand and gave me a glass full of hot liquid, sticky and overly sweet. I drank the entire contents of the glass, loudly sucking up the foam at the bottom.

"Give him another glass!"

I drank three glasses like this, one after another. Then they helped me eat a bit of dried meat sprinkled with butter. In the shade, my field of vision had enlarged and now included a deep, circular porthole that encompassed the tree and its surroundings within a portion of the luminous blue sky. He started to speak to me, first in an incomprehensible language, then in perfect, classical Arabic. He asked me all sorts of questions about myself and the reasons for my presence at the top of this mountain. I wanted to answer him and tell him that I didn't know who I was or why I was here, but I kept silent in spite of myself. He tried to communicate with me through gestures, without any further success, and ended up giving up, leaving me stretched out in the shade, near his Venus who had calmed down by now.

He gave orders about how to pack the baggage and load it up on the camels that the *tirailleurs* had brought back. The large metal trunks and kegs were arranged in half-loads with the saddletrees. "*Wetch! Wetch!*" cried the men as they tried to get the camels to kneel. Before loading up the pack camels, the saddletrees made of arched wood were placed on top of thick rolls of padding which were folded in half in front of the hump. Another camel was harnessed with a palanquin topped with hoops and a dais covered by a comfortable canopy—a sort of mobile pavilion draped all around in white cloth decorated with strips of red, yellow, and blue. Two riding camels wore the Méharist harnesses of the camel cavalry; one had an old, worn-out saddle and the other had a new, well-padded, and comfortable saddle. The goatskins, some limp, some swollen and dripping with water, were hung up by their legs and dangled under the kegs. Ghostbuster ordered the *tirailleurs* to carry me over and put me on the pack camel that carried the smallest load. He told Mardoucha to mount with me to keep me from falling. Then they untied the hobbles around the knees of our mount and got it to its feet. They checked the reins and the chin straps and then had the other pack camels stand up. I was now lying on my side, almost three meters in the air, held securely by a copper-skinned man. The beasts bleated and shifted under their still unstable burdens. Ghostbuster made the rounds, checking on the tie-downs and balancing the loads. The camel with the canopy and the one with the comfortable saddle remained kneeling. When the line of pack camels had been roped together behind the Méhari camel with the old, worn-out saddle, Ghostbuster called out, "Galgala, run and get Vala. Tell her that her camel is ready!"

My eyes followed him as he ran. He found her atop a dune, facing the full sun, leaning toward the horizon to see if a hospitable face could be seen. She stayed there a moment, then came back toward us, walking ahead of him. Galgala arrived at the same time as she did, and, kneeling, he hunched over against the left shoulder of the camel carrying the pavilion, offering his back as a footstool; Ghostbuster offered his arm. She hitched up her veil, placed her bare right foot on Galgala's back and hoisted herself up, holding on to Ghostbuster's shoulder while he took hold of her right foot and raised her up. With one leap, she was inside her canopy in the middle of her cushions. The last two camels were made to stand and join the line, and the convoy headed off toward the southeast.

The heat had eased a little, but the sand-laden wind kept blowing just as hard. The shadows slipped furtively toward the east, as if they wanted to flee from us. The terrain promised to be very difficult. The huge sand massifs were often crisscrossed by lines of shifting dunes oriented in a slightly different direction. Traces of the trade wind from the northeast and the monsoon from the south were imprinted upon the dunes. These formations rarely subsided and the convoy was often forced to attack the difficult massifs head-on in order to stay on course. The monotony of these extreme shapes was broken up only by a few fragmented white ergs. The men walked painfully without straying from the convoy. Only Ghostbuster veered to one side or the other and sometimes hung far behind. He seemed to be searching for something. He examined every detail along the way and stopped in certain places to pick up a rock, a bone, a shell, a shard, or something else that he carefully wrapped up before giving it to Vala for safekeeping; Vala's upper body would appear from her pavilion and reach down to take them from him. My counterweight never once stopped talking:

"I've finally found someone to talk to! I know that you hear me and are listening to me, but that you can't respond. I hate responses because they never correspond to the questions. They're always assertions that draw their reasons from something else! In any case, if you respond to me, I'll make you fall and tell Ghostbuster that it was an accident, that you slipped out from between my hands! I don't like when men speak to me because they are always stubborn and limited by their ignorance! You abstain from articulating any sound, but you are not mute, you have merely lost your speech momentarily. Shock and fear assail you. Speech eludes you. You say nothing about your great transgression! As for me, people have shut my mouth too often for me not to take advantage of a guy like you! When I cried out at my birth, they shut my mouth! In military school, they forbade me to speak unless someone told me I could and the sergeant put me on work duty any time I spoke while in line! In civilian life, you can't complain 'cause it's not polite, and besides, since I'm neither rich, nor well-born, I have no right to speak! When I can speak, I always end up with someone who's hard of hearing or jabbering mouths instead of ears! The moment I utter a sound, Being deserts its house, and when I dream of wonders from a far-distant land, my demon invariably tells me: 'Nothing of the sort slumbers in the depths of the valley!"

Not only had I remained silent, but I had also closed my eyes, fearing that this maniac would throw me overboard, under the hooves of the camel following behind us. The swaying as we went up and down the slopes, along with the long litany of my counterweight ended up putting me to sleep.

And then, I recovered my past identity and consciousness as a time-traveler. I wondered what era I was in.

Perhaps I haven't changed eras. The sun, the wind, and the sands of the Great Desert are still just as impassive. There are still men with their camels in a caravan, masters and slaves, as always. Have I been duped by the Green One who guards the sea of time? Yet this caravan seems rather strange to me; it is too different to be from the same era as the caravan to Sijilmasa…That Raving Logophile who serves as my counterweight would turn a good profit at the Awdaghost marketplace… And Vala! How she has changed! And I frighten her now! How could she have come to be here in this caravan with this Ghostbuster guy? Is it another woman with the same name? But what an uncanny resemblance, especially the look in her eyes! I will speak to her as soon as I wake up; I'll remind her of our long nights in Awdaghost, in the abandoned house in the craft district. I'll ask her for news of the slave uprising…

I woke up with a start, between the sky and the earth, less than a meter from the ground, and fell down hard, sinking deep into the soft sand. Startled by my fall, the camel kicked its hind legs out, breaking the chin strap tying it to the one I was riding, thus saving me from being trampled.

I cried out, "He did it on purpose!"

All at once, everyone said, "He spoke! He spoke!"

I leaned on the guy who had come to help me and stood up, taking a few steps before falling again.

"He's walking! Ghostbuster! He spoke! He walked!"

Ghostbuster came over to us.

"He did it on purpose," I said again, this time to Ghostbuster. "He threatened me. I was sleeping when he pushed me off!"

"I swear I didn't mean to! The slope was too steep—he slipped right through my hands!"

"Imbecile! You'll be on work duty tonight and tomorrow!" Ghostbuster snapped at him in an angry and scornful voice.

The moon was shining, lighting up the gentle curves of sand which seemed to be animated by a feminine spirit. Ghostbuster gave the order to pitch camp for the night at the bottom of a depression, between two high, rounded dunes. There were a few meager *ɡfar* and some rather sparse clumps of camel grass. The camels were unloaded and hobbled tightly, and we settled down for the night. The copper-skinned man—my counterweight who had betrayed me—managed to gather a few dried-out tufts and lit a small fire whose dancing flames shed new light on the desolate moonlit camp. Mardoucha hastily prepared the dried meat and sprinkled it with melted butter. Then he heated the tea and quickly served Ghostbuster and Vala, who had retired to be near the canopy now resting on the ground. After the tea, when the camp had surrendered to the night and was succumbing to exhaustion, Ghostbuster called for me. Supported by Mardoucha, I stumbled over to him, my sluggish body still not completely recovered.

"That's fine, Mardoucha, you can leave him now. Sit here... that's it... So, what progress you have made, and so quickly! That fall from the camel produced a miracle—you recovered your voice, and you will soon be able to walk normally. Now, tell me about yourself."

"I know nothing of myself!"

"How is that, you know nothing of yourself?"

"You already know all that I know!"

"Who are you? Your name?"

"I don't know if I have a name! I don't know who I am or where I come from! All I know about myself is that yesterday on top of the mountain, I heard voices and footsteps approaching me, and it was the *tirailleurs* who then brought me here. I don't remember anything before that!"

His Venus, looking magical in the moonlight, had stretched out on the still-hot sand and was scrutinizing me suspiciously. To the other side, behind the trunks and kegs, some of the *tirailleurs* were already snoring. A jerboa bounded quickly and silently down from the top of the dune, the tuft of black and white fur at the end of its tail skimming the sand along the way.

"He claims he's lost his memory," said Ghostbuster to Vala.

She said nothing and rolled over to lie on her back, offering her face to the deluge of stars.

"Mardoucha! Come take him back to his place, I'll deal with his problem later."

I returned to my place and lay down again among the others, unable to sleep. I heard Vala's voice and saw Galgala run off. He ran up a dune and disappeared behind it. She went toward him and disappeared behind the crest at the same spot. When he came back to lie down in his place, I crept over to him and whispered in his ear, "What did you do when you went off together?"

"I dug her hole."

"Her hole?"

"Yes, her hole. It's my job; I am responsible for the holes of the archaeologist's mistress!"

"What a job! And so? What does it entail?"

"I admit that it's not very hard, considering the terrain here. Each time she feels the need to relieve herself, she alerts me, and I find the appropriate place to dig a nice, round hole for her, or two or even three sometimes, which I must fill back up after she has used them."

"She's really spoiled."

"You have no idea! Take, for example, the other day, at the stopover before the well at Ghallawiya. Well, because of her, we almost all died of thirst and yet we had some water."

"Really? How's that?"

"It was really hot that day. The water rations were

depleted. We had left before dawn, hoping to be at Ghallawiya before noon. But a burning wind had picked up and we were forced to stop. We were parched for the entire day. Yet there was still one keg half full of water! But Ghostbuster forbade us to drink from it. 'That water,' he said, 'is reserved for Vala's bath. I forbid you to touch it!' Luckily the guide was able to save us by taking us to the well in the middle of the night. But one *tirailleur* who was too parched died after drinking a large amount of water. We would have all died of thirst because he wouldn't let us touch his mistress's bathwater!"

"And all those huge trunks? What's in them?"

"They contain supplies for archaeological prospecting and excavating: pickaxes, trowels, wheelbarrows, shovels, cameras, measuring tools, drawing materials, topographical maps."

"Who would buy all that merchandise with such bizarre names?"

"Who said anything about selling? They are tools used for archaeological work!"

"Archaeology, is that Ghostbuster's nickname?"

"No, it's his profession. He practices archaeology; he explains the past through figured monuments. But stop bothering me! You're like a child, you ask too many questions!"

I spent part of the night unable to sleep. The sky had put on its blue coat, studded to infinity. It was as if all the peoples of all the galaxies had contributed to its adornment by each offering a sample of its most beautiful jewel.

Matalla

At departure this morning, I was able to sit up on my camel, but was still reeling a bit. Ghostbuster had a different copper-skinned man ride with me to keep me steady. The Raving Logophile walked in silence among the others. The summits of the shifting dunes were already smoking, promising another windy day, and the overly generous sun was giving us our fill of its daily rations. I was struck with a sudden longing: I wanted a good conversation, something comfortable and very ordinary; perhaps it was one of the many viruses that the Raving Logophile sowed along his path. But my new counterweight seemed far from loquacious. The one time I wanted to converse, and I couldn't have had worse luck. I wanted to feel him out anyway, before the great heat of the day tied our tongues and liquefied our brains.

"So many anachronisms as the days go by!"

"Huh?"

"Yet another windy day!" I said, correcting myself.

"It's like this all year round!"

"Why continually roam across the sand, exposed to the sun and wind?"

"It's that marker of empty places, that seeker of ghosts, who wants us to scour the entire expanse of his yearning!"

"That guy?"

"It's that ball-breaker Ghostbuster— he rounded us all up in Tichitt to bring us into the Great Desert, to track the ancient caravans. He's crazy! How can anyone find the traces of a camel walking in the sand, ten centuries later?"

"And why does he follow the traces of the ancient caravans?"

"He thinks they'll lead him to the ruins of Awdaghost, a city along the caravan route that has since vanished!"

"Awdaghost? That's so strange. That name seems familiar to me. I must have heard it somewhere before. But no! Surely, it's an illusion! Maybe it's because it sounds like Ghostbuster's name!"

The day slipped between our fingers without further ado. Soon, the caravan was nothing more than a worn-out dragon, buffeted by the waves of light upon the surface of the fiery quartz. Out in front, Vala's white pavilion floated along between the sky and the earth, like the sails of a cosmic ship. My counterweight's wellspring of words had already completely dried up and he kept his mouth tightly closed so that his tongue would not escape as well.

The sun dropped in the sky, taking with it a bit of the heat of the day. The wind, calmer now, died away. And there was immobility, respite. We stopped for the evening in a camp of addax hunters whom we had met on our way. There were two of them with their pack of energetic Sloughi dogs. They had already finished their hunt and had settled into a vast gorge strewn with carcasses where the pure air of the Great Desert, which expanded the lungs and dilated the eyes, was replaced by a stifling odor of carrion. The meat, cut into strips, was drying on the sand, between the bones and the large swollen sacks dripping with grease. The fetid odor had a soporific effect on me. I was able to fall asleep very early that night and regain my consciousness as a time traveler.

So, I've really changed eras! Al-Khadir was true to his word. My counterweight told me it's been ten centuries, and no one even knows the location of Awdaghost anymore! That short man with the large head—what a prophet! But it's not possible! Ten centuries, he said! And they don't even know where the ruins of Awdaghost are! No, it's not possible! It must just be Ghostbuster trying to compensate for his shortcomings! But as soon as I wake up, I will tell him in front of everyone that I will lead him to Awdaghost. I will tell him that I left that city less than a month ago and will describe it to him before taking him there. I'll tell him that it's located in a cirque at the base of a tall, arid, white mountain, that its houses are tall and beautiful, that it has furnaces for melting gold and making glass, along with numerous marketplaces that are always bustling with crowds so dense and racket so loud that you can barely hear what the guy next to you is saying. I'll also tell him that you meet young women there with beautiful faces, fair skin, supple bodies, perky breasts, narrow waists, broad shoulders, ample behinds, tight vaginas and that whoever is lucky enough to have one will experience as much pleasure as with a virgin in Paradise. I'll also tell him of the dangers that menace the city: the wells drying up, the deforestation of the surrounding areas,

Ibn Yasin's imminent attack, Al-Khadir who has come from beyond
time to destroy the city's furnaces, and also the slave rebellion.

I was awoken by the image of my father shaking me vigorously to take me to the salt caravan and I heard Ghostbuster's voice, sputtering with impatience.

"So? So? You know where the city is! You know its location?"

"What city?"

"The city you were talking about just a moment ago, in
your sleep!"

"I did? I spoke of a city?"

"You there, go on! Repeat to him what you heard!" he
said to a copper-skinned man standing near us.

"I was lying near him, but I wasn't sleeping. I heard him
talking about Awdaghost, saying that he was going to lead
you there. Then he started to describe it. I thought he had a
fever and was delirious, but that you might be interested in
what he was saying!"

"So, you see?" said the archaeologist, shaking me with
both hands. "You see that you were talking about Awdaghost! You know too much about this city, you could not have
invented all that! You must have read the ancient authors!
How could you have known all that information? Have you
read al-Bakri?

"Al-B...? I've never heard of this name!"

"Then how can you describe with such precision a city
that disappeared ten centuries ago?"

I professed my good faith and swore that I could remember nothing, that I had no idea about this city of Awdagost... Awdagast...

"Awdaghost!" roared Ghostbuster.

"I swear I know nothing of this city!"

Ghostbuster put his head in his hands. "How can he be completely unaware, when awake, of what he so clearly knows when he's asleep?"

Starting that night, he watched over me every night awaiting my ravings. He was always studying me with his cyclops eye while I slept.

One day, shortly after sunrise, Ghostbuster gave the order to halt and pitch camp for the day. We had only crossed a few dunes since our departure at dawn. No one understood the reason for this unexpected stop. Then, when he called for everyone to sweep away the sand, we knew that he had just discovered under a crumbling slope the fleeting impression of a bleached camel carcass. He doubled everyone's water ration, ordered us to clear off and comb through the entire dune before nightfall. The excavations didn't end until the sun was nothing more than a large grain of sand free-falling toward the horizon. But the harvest from this long day of sandy, sweaty, sunny, windy labor was nothing more than a copper ingot and a mummified sloughi dog. Ghostbuster couldn't conceal his disappointment—he thought he'd found an entire caravan washed up in the middle of the desert.

After this letdown, he started to show more interest in me than he had on the way there, as if he thought that my mind contained all the treasures he was seeking. He even rescheduled the stages so that he could meet with me one-on-one at certain times of the day.

The first time he called me for this long series of interviews, he had instructed us to pitch camp upon a summit, just before sunset. The wind had died down and the placid undulations silently longed for the sky. The heat, less intense now, had settled down into the sand as night approached. He had tucked his tunic into his baggy pants and had buried his feet in the sand. He had taken on a paternal attitude and an expression of sagacious wisdom illuminated his face. His slightly moist eyes seemed to drink from the wellspring of the West within his heart. He began by saying that he wanted to establish mutual trust between the two of us.

"I want to help you heal from your trauma. I think that your memory loss results from traumatic events that we are not yet aware of. But we are going to be able to discover them together and when we have brought them to light, you will regain your memory. But for this to happen, I'll need your active participation. Are you ready to trust me and to collaborate openly with me?"

"Of course! So, you're going to help me know who I am and where I come from?"

"That's right!"

"I'll do anything you want!"

The sun had set and the first stars were already rushing into the sky. Mardoucha served a second glass in which the tastes of sugar and tea were balanced in a reconciliation sealed with fire. Ghostbuster had me lie down on my back and told me to look at the stars.

"You see that bright star over there?"

"Yes, I see it!"

"Look at it and keep staring at it. Really look at that star, don't let your eyes stray from it. Concentrate all your attention on it!"

He repeated the same instructions for a long while. Then he continued in a monotone voice.

"You are now in a state of altered consciousness. You will respond to my verbal stimuli. A change is going to take place in your consciousness and in your memory. You are becoming more and more susceptible to my suggestions. You will provide responses and ideas that may be unfamiliar to you. But first, you are going to sleep, sleep, sleep! You will enter into an artificial somnambulism that will allow me to communicate verbally with you. You will sleep… asleep… asleep… You are asleep now! Tell me what you see!"

"I see the Earth ravaged by Evil! Men reduced to their basic instincts! God has removed his proof from the Earth! It's daytime, but it's as dark as night. There is nothing but darkness. An eternal night envelops the Earth. Men have turned to debauchery! Evil flourishes everywhere! The Earth tumbles and falls, far from all suns. It's getting darker and darker. And a long era of nocturnal chaos begins…"

I heard Vala calling, "Galgala! Galgala!"

I turned over and saw Ghostbuster sitting there, leaning over me.

"Shit!" he said. The spell had been broken.

"Huh?" I said, surprised by his vulgar language.

"It's not important; we'll try another time. You can go sleep now!"

When we left that morning, I said that I wouldn't ride, but instead preferred to walk with the others. I wanted to stretch my legs and feel the cool sand beneath my feet before the sun rose. I walked near the Raving Logophile who wasn't opening his mouth this morning. A sea of ocher was already drowning out the horizon to the east and the dunes had taken on the same color, like chameleons, and before long, the glorious sun appeared upon its ship of light, bringing order to all this nocturnal chaos. The dunes, laid bare, wept black tears that seeped away in long trails toward the west. The slopes were slightly dissymmetric, steeper on the northwest sides than on the southeast sides. The shifting dunes slanted away from the framework of the massifs. But most of the time, we followed wide, endless, parallel valleys that held patches of vegetation, predominantly *sbot*. Soon, my feet began to hurt. Ever since we started off, an abrasive paste made of quartz dust had rubbed the soles of my feet raw. Grains of sand got stuck in the abrasions and made walking more and more painful. I ended up sitting down and telling Ghostbuster that I could no longer walk. He ordered Galgala to let me ride with him. So Galgala jumped down to kneel his camel and fell awkwardly to the ground, crying out in pain— he had twisted his foot and they had to lift him up to help him remount.

At the midday stop, Ghostbuster called for me.

"You are going to replace Galgala in serving Vala," he said distractedly, counting the shards he had gathered along the way.

I had barely started eating my bowl of dried meat when I heard Vala call.

"Matalla! Matalla!"

I lowered my face back to my meat, thinking she was calling one of the *tirailleurs*. But she continued to call and no one responded. So, I ran to her to find out what she wanted.

"Well, now! That took a while! Why didn't you come when I called?"

"I thought you were calling for someone else!"

"No! It was you whom I was calling!"

"But I thought I heard you say Matalla."

"You are not mistaken! Matalla, which means Given by God, is the name I have given you. Now hurry up and carry my bath water behind that dune over there and wait for me!"

I was behind the dune for a long time. Beside me was the bucket full of water, reflecting the sun. I heard no sound, only a sidereal silence. I no longer saw the camp; there was nothing but sand as far as the eye could see, everywhere, and fiery waves gliding swiftly across the surface. I started to doubt the reality of Vala, the camp, and myself. If it hadn't been for the bucket full of water mirroring the sun upon its surface, whose reality I could test by dipping my hand in, I would have thought that it was all nothing but an illusory dream. Then, I saw her upon the crest and she quickly approached me.

"Get to the side while you wait for me to finish," she said, placing a chunk of soap near the bucket.

She removed her veil without waiting for me to move away and appeared naked in the sunlight. *What a beauty this archaeologist's mistress is! I could never have imagined that her veil concealed such perfect curves!* I drew back even further down the crumbling slope, aroused, glancing at her out of the corner of my eye, not daring to look at her directly. She first poured a little water on her body before taking the piece of soap and carefully running it over the entire surface of her skin, then she set it down and began rubbing her limbs with slow and harmonious movements. I saw a little fox with huge ears sneaking up to her, gliding across the sand. She had her back turned and couldn't see it. It had cream-colored fur with brownish-red spots along its back and white rings streaked with black circling its eyes. I yelled, "Watch out!" to Vala, running toward the animal. But in one leap, the fennec fox was next to her, and, sinking its teeth into the piece of soap, it took off like lightning and vanished into the sand. I wanted to follow it, but Vala had come over to snuggle up against me, crying out in terror. Through her tears, she lamented, "It took my last piece of soap, what a monster! What will I do now, in the middle of this awful desert, without soap?"

Then she abruptly removed herself from my arms and cried, "What are you waiting for, Matalla? Hurry up and catch it to get back my soap!"

It was easier said than done; I was completely numb and heard angels singing in paradise!

"Go on! Run and catch it! What are you waiting for?" I started to run after it, halfheartedly.

In order to recover her soap, I would have to find the entrance to the burrow of that accursed, ubiquitous fennec fox, whose footprints were already starting to be erased by the wind. Then, I would have to follow Allen's rule and shape-shift into a field mouse, enter the tunnels of the burrow, and search through them to find the main room. There, the fennec fox will be busy playing with the scrap of soap, unless he's already eaten it. When he sees a mouse come into the main room of his burrow, he'll tell himself that it must be his day—first the naked body of the caravan girl, then this fragrant bit of soap, and now the plump field mouse at the entrance to the main room of his burrow. Then, I'll remember my new state as a rodent and I'll try to flee, but it will be too late. The fennec fox will have already caught me, crushing my skull between his canines.

I shivered as if waking up from the middle of a nightmare. A *tirailleur* was calling me from the top of a dune, waving his arms up and down. I went back to him, relieved that I hadn't yet turned into a field mouse at the entrance to the main room of a fennec fox's burrow.

"Come on! Hurry up! Ghostbuster orders you to come back immediately. We're waiting for you to leave!"

"What about Vala's soap? I haven't yet found the fennec fox."

"You're stark raving mad! How can you find a fennec fox in the middle of the desert, in this sun and wind? It's like your siesta, the other day, on the top of Mount Ghallawiya!"

Vala Mint Bou Garn

The guide prostrated himself in an endless prayer. An ambient dull roar filled the galactic calm of the Great Desert. We were getting ready to sleep. Each man had taken his place for the night, the *tirailleurs* and lighter-skinned guys together on one side; Galgala and myself in our corner, and farther away, next to their waiting cot, Ghostbuster and his mistress. The archaeologist had moved the glowing lamp close to him and, his pen in hand, had opened a thick notebook. Vala came and rested her head against his shoulder and, looking at the open notebook, asked what he was doing.

"I'm writing!"

"And during this time, who will take care of me?" she asked, annoyed.

"But it's about you that I write, my dear!"

"How so, about me?"

"Of course, about you! It's your story that I write, a story in which you are the main character."

"Oh! Fantastic! Read it to me. I want to hear what you've written about me!"

"But… it's not finished yet."

"That doesn't matter! I want to hear what you've already written. Come on! I'm begging you!"

"Okay, okay… It starts one evening, during the time when they were force-feeding you: *The full moon rose up and broke away from the horizon, like a menace hovering over the earth, still a bit red, ashamed to show itself to the face of the world so soon after the blazing sun had set. The moon seemed fearful that the sun would rise back up in front of it, as promised in the myth about the end of the world. Your drenched mouth remained inside the heavy calabash filled with camel's milk; it was so difficult to hold up in your hands, but you could not get rid of it under the stern gaze of your black nursemaid as she gorged you and held your foot between the zayar vice clamp which might close at any moment. To avoid this torture, you pretended to drink the milk, but in reality, only touched your lips to it while gazing intensely at the moon, intrigued by the spots on its surface. You thought they looked like the letters you tried so hard to make sense of, like an exegeses teacher studying those mysterious letters that unlocked certain verses in the Quran. Suddenly you felt your foot being crushed between the jaws of the zayar vice and felt an atrocious pain, like a wild beast caught in a cruel trap, and your eyes fell upon the hopelessly full calabash.*

'So, Vala! You think that you can fool me? Are you going to keep me up all night because you refuse to drink your milk?' shouted Rayhana, squeezing even harder.

You held back a cry and almost let go of the calabash. Milk trickled from your mouth and chin down your throat and onto your chest, making white streaks on your melhfa. 'I beg you, Rayhana, let me breathe a little, just for a moment. You know that I'm on my

111

seventh calabash. I feel like I'm going to throw up if I keep drinking.'

'Keep drinking and be quiet! Too bad if you puke!' said Rayhana in a no-nonsense tone, pinching your thigh painfully. So, you plunged your open mouth back into the milk and forced yourself to drink as much as you could, hoping to feel the vice loosen on your foot.

Under the black camel-hair tent, lit only by rays of moonlight, you cursed your destiny. You envied the carefree, innocent sleep of your two younger brothers, lying naked on the corner of the mat. Why wasn't I born a boy? Why are girls force-fed and not boys? If only my mother was here, she could order Rayhana to let me breathe a little! Your mother had left the household after an argument with your father, Bou Garn. She had gone to live in her parents' tent. Your father had begged her to return; he had even resorted to the mediation of the two most important matrons of the encampment, but your mother had remained obdurate. This morning, one of the matrons had come to see your father to tell him that his wife would agree to come back, but that, as a gift of reconciliation, she demanded jewels from Oualata. Your father's initial reaction was to protest, 'She's being unreasonable! Where am I going to find these jewels? No one sells them here and Oualata is in the Hodh region, at the other end of the world!'

'Figure it out. You must know that the reconciliation gift your cousin Shannane gave his wife was much more rare!'

'That's what ruining us all—everyone always has to do more than his cousin, even if he is unable to!'

'Don't go flouting our traditions—you know that a reconciliation gift is mandatory!'

'I know, I know. But I don't understand why she left!'

'She's acting like the other women; she must quarrel with her husband from time to time to test his love for her!'

'That's totally absurd!'

Manu, your father's griot, woke his master up every morning with jarring music played energetically on his lute, using mostly re-la chords. Invariably dressed in a white boubou made of percale and a guinea cloth turban, Manu was more than fifty years old and had mastered his art to perfection. That particular day, when your father woke up, Manu was still playing makka musa, starting in the karr mode, played in the white Way, a horizontal composition centered on the tonic sol and in which the dominant re-fa# is ever-present. A young slave girl was preparing the tea, heating it over a clay stove full of charcoal embers. She served the first glass and Bou Garn drank it in one gulp. The bitter taste of the green tea roused his sense of pleasure and his will to power. He made the decision to form a raiding party that he himself would lead on an expedition to Oualata.

'Manu, go announce to the entire tribe that I'm leaving tomorrow on an expedition to the Hodh region. Have all volunteers gather tomorrow at dawn in front of my tent, ready to depart!' He called for Matalla, his strongest slave who accompanied him in all his raids. 'Matalla, go find the two best méhari camels in the herd. We leave tomorrow before the break of day!'

Venus was still peacefully shining with all her charming radiance when about thirty men, riding beautiful camels and armed with lances, swords, and rapid-fire guns, gathered in front of Bou Garn's tent. Their well-trained mounts were silent, obedient to the reins and used to kneeling on only their back legs to allow for a quicker ascent into the saddle. Each rider had his camel harnessed and a provision of water, dried meat, and tea. Standing in the middle of the camel

riders, Manu was singing a long poem of great praise in a loud voice,
stirring them to war. With his lute, he was playing sruzi in the faghu
mode, following the white Way. This melodious structure roused the
enthusiasm and expressed great strength. When Bou Garn gave the
signal to depart, the raiding party took off at a gentle trot, singing the
song of departure. The men looked behind them and mocked the lazy
ones who had stayed behind:

'Woe to every woman,
Whose man prefers taking his ease:
Before the fire warming his knees,
Drinking his watered-down milk!'
They asked God to bring them back to their family and friends:
'Her prayers and fasting never cease,
Consulting her fate more than ever!
May God bring us back together,
As long as I return in one piece!'

Bou Garn had not yet returned. You were alone with Rayha-
na and your little brothers who were already asleep, and you had to
drink more gourds full of milk. The night was hot, the air heavy with
humidity. An oppressive heat enveloped the encampment, like it had
every evening during the entire winter stay, which had been partic-
ularly rainy that year. The firelight in front of the tent was attracting
swarms of insects.

The muezzin was calling for the Isha prayer when the sky turned
dark. The moon was obscured by a thick black wall that brought the
sky down to the earth. The wind picked up, growing stronger and
wilder; bolts of lightning stabbed the horizon, surreptitiously shedding
light on the woes of the world. Thunder rumbled ominously. A violent
wind blew over the encampment. The rain began to fall. For an

instant, the earth looked as it did before mankind. The wind stirred up violent whirlwinds of dust that swept up everything in their path. All the tents were blown over; disorder and panic reigned throughout the camp. The storm had surprised everyone; they hadn't had the time to take down the tents. Men cried out, children wept, women commended themselves to God. And when a lightning bolt illuminated this chaos, you were thrilled to see the overturned calabashes and the milk draining out onto the sand. You were delighted to notice that Rayhana had forgotten about you and you implored the storm to keep going: 'Zidi! Zidi! More! More!' The tumult was exacerbated by the doleful braying of the beasts wandering aimlessly among the tents, wounded by the thorny branches of the calf enclosures, now tossed about by the wind.

The wind died down and the rain stopped abruptly. Everyone started setting up the tents again, searching for the herds, and relighting the extinguished fires in the hopes of drying out a bit before the sun rose. And to your great relief, you spent the rest of the night with no more milk, since they were not able to gather up the herds that night.

Each tent had its own animals, with some families possessing more than others, according to their place in the tribal hierarchy. Bou Garn, the chief of the tribe whose name he shared, was the most wealthy man in terms of beasts and slaves. He owned two herds of cattle, three herds of sheep and goats, and a herd of camels. Grouped around his tent were six burlap tents for the ten or so families of slaves that had been passed down from father to son for several generations. Rayhana was the most devoted and the most faithful of these slaves. Bou Garn also had his family of griots, the Manus, famous through-out Barzakh for their mastery of Moorish music and poetry. They were the keepers of the tribe's tradition and glory. The Bou Garn tribe led their nomadic life across an expanse of almost two thousand kilometers between Zemmour and Hodh.

You were awoken by your Quran teacher. You had barely slept for two hours from the end of the storm to the beginning of your first lesson. You rubbed your eyes, barely making out the silhouette of Hamed as he lit a small wood fire in front of the tent. Dawn was breaking on the horizon, blotting out the less brilliant clusters of stars. It was time for the first prayer of the day, the morning prayer. Hamed went into the tent to get water for his ablutions and came back with a kettle in his hand. He knelt, sitting on his heels and facing the east, washed his hands meticulously three times, rinsed out his mouth three times, then his nose, his face and forearms; he rubbed his moistened hands back and forth across his head and washed his ears and feet, the right foot first and then the left foot. He remained for a moment with both hands clasped in front of his face, eyes closed, moving his lips in inaudible prayer. Then he got up and sang out the call to morning prayer.

By the time the closing lines of the prayer were said, the light had taken possession of the earth. The pale morning revealed the surface of things, promising a new day, one more, and one less in the life of every being.

'Vala, come recite your surahs!' said the Quran teacher in his commanding and threatening voice. You stumbled out of the tent and began the first verse in a voice still groggy from sleep. 'Invoke God against Satan and enunciate!' said Hamed, waving his whip over you. This threat chased off all your remaining sleepiness. You invoked God and continued your recitation with your very best enunciation. The slaves bustled around the animals, milking them before leading them out to the grazing areas, far from the camp. The first rays of the

sun were already peeking up over the horizon.

The Quran teacher was preparing to write out the lesson for the day. He held a stalk of gramineae in his hand, whittling it to a sharp point with his knife. When it was the shape of a plume, he made a small slit in it. 'Bring me your lawh and the ink pot,' he instructed you. You went into the tent without interrupting your recitation. You reached under the palanquin for the earthenware ink pot and the writing board made from aglal wood and brought them to your teacher. The writing board was completely covered in writing on both sides, and a layer of dried black ink coated the bottom of the ink pot. Hamed washed both sides of the lawh in a wooden bowl to erase the previous writing and placed it delicately on his right thigh, before drinking the water left over from the washing: this water was sacred and must be consumed each time—throwing it away amounted to sacrilege. He poured a bit of water into the inkpot, took a chunk of acacia charcoal, and began to dissolve it by vigorously rubbing it against the bottom of the pot. Then, he took a chunk of gum resin and dissolved it in the same way. This mix of water, resin, and acacia charcoal produced a perfectly black ink. The Quran teacher placed the lawh on his left leg, took the plume in his right hand, dipped it into the ink, and began to write out the lesson of the day.

The herds were already leaving the encampment to the hoarse shouts of the shepherds, and the chanting of children coming from every corner of the camp indicated the first Quran lesson of the day. You had already finished reciting your lesson from the previous day. Now you were reading your lesson of the day out loud again and again and wouldn't stop until you had memorized it perfectly. The teacher listened to you and harshly corrected you any time you made a mistake.

Now the kettle whistled on the fire. Hamed picked up the leath-

er sack with a stiff bottom to carry the teapot and glasses, a round bas-
ket covered with an embellished animal hide, and with a collar of soft
leather painted with matching decorations, each side having a central
pattern encircled by smaller patterns in red, yellow, and blue; from the
base of the collar hung leather fringe, some very narrow, others wider
and covered in designs; the collar was scalloped with a delicate strip of
animal hide. He took out the teapot and placed it on the copper platter
decorated with silver designs and arranged the glasses in a semi-circle
around the teapot. You brought the sugar and the green tea. For a moment, Hamed lost track of the Quran verse you were reciting, dreaming instead of this verse from the poet Habib: 'Before the sun, already
rising up from the earth toward the sky, I hurry to make a light tea.'

He took one of the little glasses from the semi-circle, filled it
two-thirds full with green tea, poured its contents back into the teapot, added a bit of simmering water, and shook it vigorously before
emptying it all into a glass, thereby aerating the tea for the first time,
and then poured a larger amount of boiling water into the teapot and
placed it on the coals for a brief moment before removing it and adding
a piece of crushed sugar. He poured the tea several times back and forth
between the teapot and the glasses to thoroughly mix the tea and the
sugar. He put the teapot back on the fire for a moment before pouring
the tea. In it, he could taste a bitter flavor vying with a sweet one, but
both persisted without drowning the other out. The bitter flavor clearly
dominated the taste of the first glass, but its triumph presaged its fall in
the second and third glasses.

You liked this drink whose color resembled the color of henna
and liked to watch the variations in its color: the red of the first glass,
the golden red of the second, and the gold color of the third. The crown
of froth that sparkled in the glasses always reminded you of the crown

of white hair on an old bald man. You really wanted to taste the delicious, hot drink that your teacher was preparing, but you dared not ask for any: tea was forbidden to young women. However, on rare occasions, you had dared to taste this forbidden drink, but always in secret or in the company of the slaves.

The sun set slowly before sinking down into the sea of sand. The shadows stretched out disproportionately, abandoning their source, which was no longer but a memory. It was the time of day when the young women of the camp could come out and get together. Each day, they took advantage of this moment of freedom to go far away from the encampment, away from the watchful eyes of the adults. And the boys came to join them there. You always looked forward to this time of day. When you turned fourteen, this time had taken on a new significance; you had come to realize the meaning behind the boys' desirous looks and understand the agitation that your presence stirred in them. You had picked up the habit of listening to their compliments with well-disguised indifference. Occasionally you deigned to thrill one or another of the boys with a look, all the while laughing at the rivalry your interest created among them. Your mother had advised you to never be sincere with men. She often said to you, 'If you love a man, never show him! Feign love when there is no love and feign the absence of love when there is love—that's the secret to woman's power over man!' But you dreamed of a man with whom you could always be sincere, a man to whom you could say, 'I love you!' and who would calmly respond, 'I know!'…"

"I was dreaming of you!" said the character to her author.

"… *Since there was no one in the tent at that moment, you de-cided to make yourself pretty before going out. You opened your mother's jewelry box, took a mirror, and held it up in front of your face. A bit of kohl would make the contrast between the white and black parts of your eyes even more striking. You took a smooth, polished lead stick out of the box, opened a little leather sack containing a piece of kohl, rubbed the end of the merwad over the kohl, and ran it along the edge of your eyelids, at the base of your eyelashes. Your eyes admired your eyes and got lost in the contrast of their beauty.*

The slow, melancholy afternoon flowed imperceptibly into eternity, giving an insubstantial consistency to each thing, as if it was going to waste away in a wistful sigh. You left the encampment and headed west, following the sun in its solitary quest for some welcoming face. When you arrived at the top of the first dune behind the camp, you saw the tight knot of girls and boys further down the dune, without being able to make out their faces. They were in a circle around one of the young women, who were all wearing black and easily distinguished from the boys. The color and shape of their veils made a sharp contrast with the blue and white boubous that the boys wore; some of whom also wore turbans the same color as the girls' veils. Seeing you approach, three of the boys left the group and came to greet you. Now, you could clearly make out the light music of an ardin harp, the instrument reserved for women in the system of Moorish music. The young woman in the middle of the group was Mounnina, the oldest of Manu's daughters. She was sitting down, the neck of the harp resting on her left shoulder, supported between her thumb and the palm of her hand. Her other free fingers plucked the strings of the instrument that she played with both hands. Resting on the ground in front of her was the body of the instrument: half of a spherical calabash about fifty cen-

timeters in diameter, with sheepskin stretched across it and little bells attached to the top to create a metallic jingling sound. Fourteen strings formed a plane perpendicular to the sound table and were strung between the neck of the harp and a piece of wood mounted horizontally across the sound table at an obtuse angle that made it possible to play any piece of music in any of the traditional modes, without having to tune the instrument. The young griot played a white music, pleasant and simple, enveloping the group in an atmosphere of love and melancholy, giving ardent expressions to their faces and liquefying their warm and limpid looks. Mounnina accompanied her harp with an entertaining poem of love and pleasure, a gentle and pleasing song:

'I am inexorably drawn to wherever you are.

I am perpetually in search of you.

But you reject me each time.

You claim that we are not from the same species.

That our souls are not in harmony.

Yet, there is what is.

And what all the books and all the traditions say:

God created us and we are both descendants

Of Adam and Eve, our mother.

I saw your veil slip down.

Your naked arm, all your femininity.

And a violent tumult shook my being.

I'm only obeying the urges that your being provokes within me!'

The shadows grew shorter, rapidly approaching their source, and the hot, dry wind—very bad for the pastureland—blew steadily, bringing with it ticks and forcing the men to cover their faces. You were *drinking your last calabash of the morning, under the watchful eyes of Rayhana. In the shade, people immobilized by the heat observed each other as if looking in a mirror. Waves of heat and blinding light flowed between the tents of the camp like an ocean of fire. With the heat, each movement stretched out indefinitely, as if in slow-motion. The air became liquid, making everything appear to be underwater. In the distance, you recognized your father, riding his white camel at the head of his raiding party. When he reached the tent, he got down, leaving his camel to the slaves who had come running up to meet him. One of them untied the big sack of soft leather decorated all over with red and black patterns from the back of the camel, near the crupper, before relieving the camel of its saddle and padded cushion; another led it out of the encampment and hobbled it to prevent it from wandering too far off. Rayhana was already preparing the tea.*

The return of the raiding party caused a great commotion throughout the camp. Roused from their torpor, children and slaves ran in every direction between the tents. All this excitement stirring up the camp converged at a single point—the tent belonging to Bou Garn's parents-in-law. By the time Rayhana served the first glass, there were hardly any waves left. The weight of the sun and the heat of the wind had immobilized everyone under their tents. Lethargy reigned once again over the entire encampment. The bitter taste of the first glass eased the physical fatigue of the trip. Bou Garn became aware of the importance of voluntary effort in life and in a flash realized that, from now on, his mornings must begin with an effort of will.

After the sun had set, when the dusk prayer had already been completed and the herds had been brought back to mill around between the tents, visitors with strange mannerisms, full of hidden meanings, arrived at Bou Garn's tent: gracious matrons of ample proportions with sure words and sharp gestures; servants emitting the strong odor of a day full of labor and sunlight; children with curious eyes who were seeing beings and things for the first time. And the Manu family of griots ready with praises, bringing their musical instruments: the lute, ardin harp, and timbal. A wood fire burning in front of the tent lit up everyone's faces while a servant girl prepared the tea in a corner of the tent. Her ebony face, barely visible, expressed the age-old weariness of heavy labor, against which the keen light in her eyes hopelessly protested. All around, the earth cloaked in deep shadow gazed up at the sky adorned with stars. Sometimes one jewel pulled away and the trajectory of its fall traced a scar of light across the sky. Later, when the moon rose, its face would blot out the shadows of the earth and its spirit would animate beings and things.

The griots tuned their instruments in karr, the mode of youth, pleasure, and joy, to open the concert. The instruments and the voices gave off an impression of softened harshness, which is specific to the introduction played in the white Way. Your mother arrived flanked by two matrons. Bou Garn barely looked at her and didn't speak to her at all, in accordance with the custom. Later, when all this clamor died down, and the crowd left, leaving only the invisible imprints of their bodies in the air, he would find himself alone with her in the darkness of the tent, with their sleeping children. Then he could prove to her how happy he was to have her back. You would be there the whole time, eyes closed, but unable to sleep, forcing yourself to control your breathing as it became faster and heavier."

Ghostbuster stopped reading and put away his note-book.

"It's marvelous! I love it!"

"I'll read you the rest later."

She kissed him on the cheek and put her arms around him in a gesture of overflowing tenderness. He turned off the lamp and got into bed. Vala came and cuddled up next to him. She wriggled in his arms and giggled like a hen, panting with pleasure. The *tirailleurs* snored in concert with the wind, and my gaze, no longer blinded by the light, was entirely devoted to the sky above my head.

The Sandstorm

The sandy wind was still blowing as strong as ever even though night had fallen. The meager fire of *had* shoots had gone out and the moon dimly lit up the dust-filled atmosphere. The motionless camp had surrendered to the wind.

"Damn this country!" grumbled Ghostbuster, trying to spit out most of the sand that he had inadvertently swallowed along with the last of his brackish tea.

"This is no sinecure!" replied Vala, from under her half-buried veil.

Today's stage had been particularly difficult because of the wind and the very chaotic terrain. The towering dunes were topped with huge, disorderly ergs. The stretches of *tayarets* were blocked by an inextricable tangle of shifting dunes and multiple deep basins. All this transformed the region into a steep *aklé*, slowing down the pace and making it more difficult to walk. The soft, whitish sand was predominantly garnished with *bougmiya* plants and *had* shoots. We had run across large herds of addax but hadn't disturbed them. At dawn, I noticed the ominous silhouette of Lucifer, the son of dawn, on the top of a dune. This apparition, which sent a shiver down my spine, had faded away by the time we left camp. But I was still uneasy. Just the night before I had dreamed of Ghostbuster as Beelzebub, putting salt in my eyes to make me lose my way in the Great Desert, and Vala who wanted me to submit to Allen's law and shape-shift into a field mouse. But above all, this succession of days and nights, this slow passing of perfidious time was giving me a bad feeling. And all this sand everywhere, to the left, to the right, to the back of the beyond—this raging sea, where we were completely out of place and might easily get lost, could swallow us up at any moment.

The storm lasted several days during which we didn't move an inch. It would have been madness to start walking again before it stopped. Drowning in this dark gray ocean, we could not distinguish between sky and earth, day and night, except by the fluctuations of light and temperature, freezing at night only to come to a boil again the next day. Visibility was nil and anything that didn't move was quickly submerged. Men, baggage, and beasts had been tied together along the same long rope. At regular intervals, Ghostbuster let out the same shout that sounded like a distant echo carried away by the wind. Then we roused ourselves, pulled on the rope and unearthed the buried baggage, camels, and men, before letting everything get buried all over again.

During this storm, I was tempted by the sirens of the Great Desert. I tried several times to free myself and let the wind carry me away, to melt into the sand and dissolve away once and for all. But each time, Ghostbuster felt the movement of the rope and shouted out orders to check all the anchor points one by one. The *tirailleurs* in front and behind me checked that I was still attached and tied the rope even tighter around my ankle. If only I had been placed between two half-loads or two camels, I could have escaped their vigilance and taken to the open desert.

Finally, the wind relented and died down. The storm ceased, giving the desert over to a calm immobility. The revived camp emerged slowly from the sand that had buried it, and the rope was untied. Each being and thing went back to deluding themselves that they had room to maneuver. Before sunset, the air had already regained its transparency. Our gazes were drowning in the deep blue sky, dazzling as if washed by a rainstorm. The *tirailleurs* dug in the sand to unearth a few meager *had* shoots for the fire, and Vala dusted herself off before her soap-less bath. A man with copper-colored skin brought back an addax that he had hunted down. At dinnertime, we could forgo the dried meat. We could drink a bit of sand-free tea, our mouths tasting it hesitatingly after having been duped so many times.

The next evening, when the camp had already settled down for sleep, Ghostbuster called me over "to continue our one-on-one meetings."

"Is there still trust between us?" he asked as if I had a choice.

"Yes, I trust you!"

"Lie down on your back and relax! Look at the stars and clear your mind of all thoughts. You see that bright star over there? Stare at it and concentrate all your attention on it. Don't let your eyes stray from it. You no longer see any of the other stars. You are now in a state of altered consciousness. You will respond to my verbal stimuli. A change is going to take place in your consciousness and in your memory. You are more susceptible to my suggestions. You will provide responses and ideas that may be unfamiliar to you. You will enter into an artificial somnambulism that will allow me to communicate verbally with you. You will sleep, sleep, sleep, sleep... You are asleep now!"

"No, I'm not asleep!" I said, stubbornly staying awake.

"Ok, it's not working. It's useless to keep trying. We're going to try another method. Remain lying down, relax, and close your eyes. Speak freely. Tell me everything that comes into your mind, without holding back, let your words flow unimpeded, liberated from your conscious control over them. Speak!"

"I feel unsettled! Something is weighing on my mind! It's as if there's a great windswept hole within my spirit, a feeling of lack, a hint of something unfinished, a sort of dead-end into which my consciousness has strayed! I am torn between dreams and reality, between my consciousness and my subconscious, like a coin between heads and tails! I am tossed about between two equally absurd situations, and I can't judge either one with a clear head while I'm in the other! Each one has shadowy zones that exile the other into an inaccessible dimension. I am the mirror between reality and wonderland, but a one-sided mirror that can only see from one side at a time—over which two valiant Alices are fighting and flipping over to look through the other's side! Between the two, I am a passive and involuntary consciousness, lost in somnambulistic wanderings. My life is but a waking dream, more insubstantial than my sleeping dreams. I see much more clearly while I sleep than while awake; I am awake in my sleep and asleep while awake, present but always absent! Try as I might to give myself orders in my dreams, I can't follow through once awake, but I feel a force within me at work, even though my consciousness suffers from lapses. I am tormented by so many things at the same time! The Raving Logophile who no longer says a word, I don't know what he has in store for me! And why did the Devil appear to me the other morning? What am I doing here with you, in your bizarre caravan? Why did you take me from the top of my mountain? Do you think I can lead you to Awdaghost? I know nothing of this phantom city whose name seemed so familiar to me at first, before I realized that it's only because it sounded like yours."

"And my own name, Ghostbuster, what does it mean to you?"

"Ghostbuster symbolizes for me the Other, the legislator, the founder of the forbidden, the taboo, the marker of empty places, the father who creates the void, the castrator!"

"And what else? What type of place does my name make you think of?"

"It makes me think of a vast arena full of slaves and spacious mansions slumbering in the shade of their gardens, of a city completely full of incense fumes and prayers mingled with children crying and old people dying of thirst!"

"So, my name makes you think of Awdaghost?"

"Awdaghost… Awdaghast… Ghost… Ghostbuster…"

"Tell me about your dreams!"

"My dreams… Too often I forget them… but some of the recurring ones leave a few lingering memories… Are you going to explain my dreams to me?"

"I wouldn't know any more than you what your dreams mean. I will not interpret them myself; I will let you recall and analyze the content of your dreams in order to understand them. But you must keep in mind that through every silence, it is the speech of the other that is propagated and that must be heard. Now, tell me what you remember about your dreams."

"The other night I dreamed that I was lighting a great fire in a deep basin. When nothing remained but ash, I gathered up some of the ashes into Vala's veil and brought them to her while she was taking her bath. But when she saw the ashes, she became enraged and poured them over my head! There is another curious dream that torments me more than any other: I dream that I split in half, that I become two, like those unicellular organisms that multiply by division. It starts with my head splitting into two, and then my arms become four, followed by my chest, abdomen, and legs. Then, the two halves run away from each other and I rush around between the two frantically trying to reunite them. But it's a hell of a task! When I gather my heads and arms together, my legs and abdomens run off again, and vice versa. My efforts to forcibly stick my parts back together sometimes result in absurd combinations: I might have, for example, a round figure with rounded back and sides, four hands, as many legs, two absolutely identical faces atop a round neck, and on the two opposing faces, one single head, four ears, and two reproductive organs, and it's like that with the rest of my body. I walk upright like normal, in any direction I wish to go, and when I start to run fast, I'm like those acrobats who twirl around kicking their legs into the air, and I spin around in a circle, supported by my eight limbs. I try to put myself into separate pieces to reattach my parts into the right position and I start by reassembling each half. But as soon as they are put together, they each run off to opposite sides, fleeing their double! Neither feels the need for the other and both foil my attempts to reunite them. In my despair at being nothing more than an invisible imprint caught between the two, I end up finding the magic formula and when I utter it, my doubles come together and start to merge into one. When everything except my legs have merged, I wake up and from the two, I become one again.

"Sometimes, I dream that I am accompanying you on a long journey, in an unknown land, upon a long road paved with salt, and when I get too tired to continue, I stop and tell you that I want to go back home. Then you hit me very hard and tie my hands with a rope and drag me along while pissing in my face. During the storm, the same dream kept haunting me: with a sturdy rope coiled around my shoulder,

I wander through the Great Desert searching for Vala's soap. A fennec fox appears at the top of a dune and I hunt it down. And when I catch it, I start to strangle it with my rope, but when it stiffens, I am horrified to discover that it's you I have strangled, that I mistook you for the fennec fox. I bury you in the sand and go back to the camp to take your place next to Vala!"

"What do you remember about your father?"

"My father? I have no memory of him. I'm not even sure if I ever had a father!"

"Yet you seem to dwell on the symbolic image of the Father. This image seems to bring up traumatic events for you."

"What traumatic events?"

"That's what we're trying to find out. That's enough for tonight; you can go sleep now!"

I was still starry-eyed when the other valiant Alice prevailed, thereby restoring my identity. I became aware of my existence beyond time and found the answers to many of Ghostbuster's questions. I promised myself to tell him the name of my father as soon as I woke up:

Fara Moul! How could I have forgotten my father's name? And if Ghostbuster wants traumatic events, I've got plenty to give him. There's no shortage of those with what I've gone through. First, there's my own birth, by far the most traumatic event of my existence— a monumental mistake that I'll never forgive myself for! Then, there's my father who sold me into slavery! There's also the failure of our

132

uprising in Awdaghost! And that caravan with masters and slaves, wandering endlessly through the Great Desert. To think that I've fled across nine centuries and still haven't managed to escape it! That Green One who guards the sea of time is having me run in circles for nothing! What's the point of changing eras if men will always be despicable bastards? Unless, much farther in the future... But I didn't want to leave Ghostbuster's hell yet; I wanted to lead him to his ghost's tomb, see the ruins of Awdaghost with my own eyes, and meditate upon the vanity of men... I would have to flee into the desert, die on the top of a mountain for good, and reject this grotesque comedy, but I told myself, 'Stay a bit longer, see everything you can see!' And I settled down to prolong this absurd slice of my life and challenged myself to find out what happens next. Besides, I doubted that I would be able to choose. This place or elsewhere? Wake up, sleep, or die? It doesn't matter that I want it definitively. It happens, that's all. I know nothing of what the future has in store for me. I cannot choose. My fate is sealed.

When I awoke, I found that I was still completely unknown to myself, unaware of my identity, totally cut off from the past, unable to remember. No matter how firmly I gave myself orders in my dreams and how determined I was to carry them out, I could never follow through in my waking state—I didn't even remember them. Beneath my conscious behavior, there was only a pretense of will. I didn't know who I was and my underlying motives were beyond me; my thoughts and my actions were but an absurd dream!

When we left in the morning, I noticed that the sand

formations were much more subdued. The folds were at once more extensive and more symmetrical, yet less prominent. The slopes of the dunes were less steep, curving down into wide valleys, where the *had* grew abundantly. The sand was deep, and the ergs had disappeared, so walking was easier. The afternoon stage was shorter than usual. We pitched camp upon a summit as the sun was just beginning to set. Shadow and light competed for the contours of the Great Desert, whose face had become hospitable. In the transparent, motionless air, the slopes were laid bare, dying away after the sun's embrace. Ghostbuster went off alone with Vala to the highest point and called for me to join them. I approached them with a heavy heart. Vala was sitting next to him, watching the sun.

"Sit down here, facing me," she said authoritatively.

I sat down facing her, slightly lower down along the burgeoning slope, so that the sun was still shining in her eyes. Ghostbuster watched us in silence.

"Now, look at me; gaze into my eyes; don't look at anything else but my eyes!"

I lost myself in her pale, luminous eyes, like the sky washed by a rainstorm. I couldn't tell if she was looking back at me or if she was watching the sun. Reflected in her black pupils, I saw the fiery disk falling gently toward the horizon. She continued to lull me with her monotone voice.

"You are gazing into my eyes; keep looking at them! You are focusing all your attention on them; you are no longer thinking of anything else! Now you are in a state of altered consciousness. A change will take place in your consciousness and in your memories. You are more susceptible to my suggestions; you will answer my questions; you will formulate ideas that are not normally familiar to you. You will enter into an artificial somnambulism that will allow me to communicate verbally with you. You will sleep, sleep, sleep…"

When I woke up, the lamp was lit, and Ghostbuster was scribbling madly in his notebook. Propped up on her elbows in the sand, Vala's face was devastated, and her eyes were red. She had rolled up her veil on her arms, like a midwife after a difficult birth. I was exhausted, emptied, incapable of moving. Ghostbuster stopped writing and put away his notebook.

"This year of 1905 will be a turning point in the history of archaeology! Colleagues will take me for a charlatan," he said to Vala huskily. "Yet everything about this testimony from beyond time fits perfectly with the information that is currently available about Awdaghost, and even fills in the details on many points, offering never-before-known information. And even if they don't believe me, the proof will be there. I will succeed where they have failed; I will discover the ruins of Awdaghost. I will show them photos of the entire topographical map of the site. And they won't be able to dispute that glory!"

He kissed Vala on the mouth and took her in his arms.

"Thank you, my dear. You are the one who deserves credit for these unprecedented discoveries. Just think! I will be the first researcher to have gotten a hold of a being from beyond time! Not to mention the answer to the great question of Awdaghost and Ghana, which I have just discovered!"

I was intrigued. What could have happened that night to make Ghostbuster so triumphant? How could he have suddenly found the answer to the mystery of Awdaghost? I didn't see this being from beyond time that he kept talking about! And Vala, what could she have done to deserve such praise?

We took a break that day. By sunrise, two tents were already pitched at the base of the dune. I was in one with Ghostbuster, Vala, Galgala, and the guide. Ghostbuster was talking about "changing the plan" and "altering the itinerary." He was also talking about the testimony of a certain Gara. What a bizarre name! It means "outlier"! That's like having "*hamada*," "dune," or "hillock" for a name!

"This will be our new itinerary," said Ghostbuster to the guide. "We will head straight toward Tijigja in order to learn about the local traditions concerning Awdaghost and Ghana. After that, we'll continue on to Tichitt, descending the *dhar* at Imdel and following the Taskas valley, which will lead us straight to the Noudache cirque, and there, if Gara's testimony proves correct, we will find the ruins of Awdaghost. We can get new supplies and camels at Tijigja. The situation is good in that city—Coppolani has recently arrived there and is building a fort; he'll provide us with all the support we need."

I collapsed into sleep as if I hadn't slept in several days. And once I reached the dream stage, I found myself whole again, in my normal shape this time:

Gara, a being from beyond time, of course, that's me! How could I not have figured that out? How could I not recognize my own name? I had never thought about the meaning of my own name: "Outlier!" What a strange thing to be called! I had never associated my name with its meaning. 1905, Ghostbuster said! So, I really did travel through time! Nine centuries! I must have ended up telling Ghostbuster everything! How many times had I resolved to tell him about Awdaghost as soon as I woke up, yet without ever doing it! And come to think of it, I don't remember telling him anything about it. And how was he able to guess my name? I certainly didn't tell him—I didn't even know it myself. Was he visited by the Green one who guards the sea of time, who then revealed everything to him? And how is Vala mixed up in all this? Why did she lull me to sleep with her eyes and her monotone voice?

Tijigja

The city of Tijigja had been transformed into a museum of atrocities. Half-burned cadavers, left hanging from the tops of the palm trees, dangled over flaming pyres. From every direction, *tirailleurs* and partisan soldiers ran toward us, shouting.

"They've assassinated the Commissioner! They've killed Coppolani!"

"Last night they burst into the half-built outpost and shot Coppolani at point-blank range!"

"It was a visionary who assassinated him, a *sharif* it seems!"

"A follower of the Smara marabout."

"Sidi Ould Moulay Zeïn!" said a copper-skinned man in a voice choked with pain and pride.

Ghostbuster was petrified. Up on the rooftop of a house, an old man lamented.

"We had nothing to do with the attack. You hung and burned innocent people! The soldiers raped our women and pillaged everything in the city!"

"Captain Frèrejean took over the command and let

loose the troops into the city last night in retaliation!" said one of the soldiers who came to greet us.

"And I can tell you that they have done much damage!"

"Take us to the captain!" said Ghostbuster.

He led us across the grove of palm trees to a dune near the *ksar*, on top of which the outpost—still under construction—was located. In a courtyard near the entrance, old men were laid out in the sun, hands and feet tied behind their backs, their beards shoved into the sand; some of them were injured. There, a tall man wearing star insignia came to greet us. He made a military salute to Ghostbuster.

"Captain Frèrejean!" he said gravely, before shaking the archaeologist's hand.

"This is most unfortunate!" said Ghostbuster. "Coppolani surely told you about me. I am Ghostbuster, leader of the archaeological mission that left Tichitt a little less than two months ago. Coppolani was very interested in my research on Awdaghost. I was just deeply distressed to hear the news that he was assassinated last night! With him gone, I lose the only man who has followed and encouraged my research since the beginning!"

"You are most welcome at Tijigja, Mr. Ghostbuster, even though you arrive at this difficult time. The late Commissioner often spoke of you and was worried when he didn't receive any news from you after you had left."

The camels were bleating and moving about restlessly as they were unloaded.

"Who are these men?" asked Ghostbuster, looking at the prisoners tied up in the sun.

"They are the city notables," said Frèrejean calmly. "I had them all arrested this morning. They will not be released until they give us the names and the hiding places of the criminals who are still on the run!"

In addition to their suffering, you could see in the eyes of these notables an unbounded pride at having seen this insane colonial dream shattered.

"So, the assassins managed to escape?"

"Some of them anyway. We don't know their exact number, but we are sure there are at least twenty of them. Never mind that; we will speak again after you have rested! Please accept my excuses for the lack of amenities, but the outpost is still under construction. We will pitch tents for you for lack of anything better!"

And he ordered his men to help get us settled in.

When I regained my own consciousness, in my dreams, that first night in Tijigja, I struggled to grasp the extent of the damage:

To travel across nine centuries and the entire Great Desert searching for Good and to end up in the middle of such injustice! It made me sick to my stomach. Into what despicable era have you taken me, al-Khadir? In the past, at least we were masters and slaves among ourselves! And Vala, what a fall from grace! To prostitute herself to the invader! It's now out of the question to express my feelings of nostalgia and sadness at the ruins of Awdaghost; I must escape this diabolical ghost seeker as soon as possible. But what should I do after that? Where can I go? I can still change eras, but it will be for the last time. I remember

al-Khadir telling me, "You will be able to stop in the first era and stay there indefinitely if you desire to. But you will also be able to leave it if it does not please you. To do that, you will simply have to retire far away from its inhabitants, as you have just done here. But this second era will be the last. You will no longer be able to escape it toward a different future and any return to the past will be impossible." So, if I leave this era, I lose my power to travel through time and run the risk of being stuck forever as a prisoner in an even worse era. Maybe it's better to stay here and help those who fight against the invader! But they might hang me and burn me like they've done to the people of Tijigja! I would then have lost my opportunity to go farther forward and perhaps find a better humanity. In any case, these invaders seem much too powerful to be pushed out! Besides, I don't trust collective endeavors ever since that traitor denounced us in Awdaghost, dooming our revolt to failure. No, no, I've seen enough already; it's pointless to wait around to see what happens next! So, let's go far into the future— perhaps there, men will be better!

When I awoke, I was still thinking about the dream I had just had. I was on the top of a mountain, praying night and day; I was hungry and thirsty and threatened by jackals and vultures. At the foot of the mountain, I saw a city with beautiful houses surrounded by gardens full of burbling water. I tried to go down to this city to quench my thirst, but at my every attempt, a short man with a large head blocked my path, preventing me from descending, endlessly repeating the same formula: "Flee from men and go into the desert!" So, I went back to pray under the watchful eyes of the vultures.

Ghostbuster asked Frèrejean to put him in contact with the scholars of the city and the keepers of oral traditions. During our stay in Tijigja, the Captain sent many men and women, mostly old ones, to our tent. Ghostbuster had meandering conversations with them about all his questions concerning the life and death of Awdaghost. They gave him contradicting versions. Some claimed that the city had been destroyed by rebelling slaves who massacred every one of their masters except two twins who were saved by their mother, because she was a concubine slave and therefore not subjected to the retribution inflicted upon her peers; others maintained that the city had been abandoned after the caravan routes were changed or as a result of the groundwater table running dry. But no one knew where the ruins of Awdaghost were located.

I often woke up thinking of the same recurring dream. I was dying of thirst on the top of a mountain; a short man with a large head prevented me from going to drink in the nearby city and kept repeating, "Flee from men and go into the desert!" After a while, I became conditioned. I decided to obey him, without knowing why. It was true that nothing was keeping me here. I was a hostage in the clutches of Ghostbuster who held me for a reason unbeknownst to me. I still didn't know who I was or where I came from, and I didn't understand why Ghostbuster was so attached to me. He called me Gara and claimed that I came from beyond time and that I had provided him with a priceless testimony about that phantom city he was seeking. I had no idea what caused him to invent such monstrous lies!

I was resolved to escape the first chance I had, to go into the desert and find that short man who haunted my dreams. But Ghostbuster put me under his watch and made me stay in his tent. He always had his eye on me, as if he knew that I wanted to escape. When he wasn't there, he posted a *tirailleur* in front of the tent. The security measures were draconian, so I stayed in the half-built fort unable to put my plan into action. I asked Ghostbuster to let me leave, but that only reinforced the surveillance that he had put in place all around me. Vala had forgotten the fennec fox and seemed to show more interest in me. Ghostbuster finished gathering the local traditions about Awdaghost and wanted to leave as soon as possible, to head toward Tegdaoust by way of Tichitt, but the captain wouldn't let him leave. He said that, with the news of Coppolani's death, the resistance fighters had gone on the offensive.

"We have to wait until reinforcements and fresh supplies arrive from Saint-Louis. An attack has taken place just south of Tijigja. A band of 80 Moors attacked a small detachment commanded by a corporal, and I just learned that the Emir of Adrar himself is heading toward Tijigja!"

Then, one day, the rescue party arrived, and our caravan was able to leave, escorted by a sergeant in charge of 17 soldiers. The wind had been blowing in from the east for three days. The scorched, dry grass on the plain caught fire. Birds of prey darted around the flames, catching insects and reptiles on the run from the wildfire. In the shade of the acacia trees, amid the swarming, ashen ticks in distress, the heat was even more unbearable than in the Great Desert. The guide had said that morning that we would be at Tichitt before night-fall. The convoy was traveling along an imposing wall of rock that ranged in color from blackish to purplish-blue, breaking up the monotony of sand stretching out to the north.

Suddenly, a hail of gunfire came from the cliff on our right and everyone hit the ground, the sergeant bellowing orders to the soldiers. I was lying down flat on my stomach behind a big black rock. Around me were dead and injured men. The artillery and the machine guns were already set up and strafing the cliffside. I saw the resistance fighters, bare-legged, with long hair and shiny eyes, leaping from rock to rock, taking cover behind the smallest obstacle, returning fire, surrounding the area— you would have thought they were veritable mountain goats. Their only weapons were their rifles, their ammunition pouches, and their daggers.

Night had fallen, lit up by the first stars and the flickers from the machine guns. A few sporadic gunshots still came from the right. I took advantage of the darkness to escape in the direction of the cliff. I climbed up the entire face without meeting a single resistance fighter. Then, I no longer heard gunfire and the desert night was restored to the calm it had known before humanity. I settled down at the top of the cliff knowing that this time, my retreat was definitive.

Part Three
The Milky Way

Prelude

"I swear never to return to this corrupt humanity and to live away from the unjust, until my death!" My new determination did not seem to have disturbed the order of the world. The sun rose and set as usual; the hot wind, heavy with sand, swirled and whistled through the mountains; and the landscape kept that same impassive expression carved into the desert sand and rock by the light and wind. But neither the torrid heat of the day nor the penetrating cold of the night, nor hunger, nor thirst had shaken my firm determination. And each time doubt started to creep into my mind, I heard the voice of that little man saying, "If you contest your destiny, flee from men and go into the desert!" Now, each passing hour was torture for my body doomed to hunger and thirst, which abated at night only to make the trial more cruel the following day.

Black vultures with powerful beaks and long, pink, featherless necks circled above, and jackals prowled around. But at regular intervals, I got up and, looking toward the east, raised my arms, hands held up on either side of my face, slightly above my shoulders, and let out a great wail that echoed and reverberated slowly across the mountains: "*Allahu akbar!*" I remained standing, motionless in prolonged expectation, murmuring my prayers. Then, I bent over, head out in front, hands pressed to my knees, with my back and legs making a right angle, then prostrated myself, forehead against the ground, then sat up, then prostrated myself again, sat up again for a moment, and stood up again with the same hoarse cry that got weaker and weaker as the hours passed. I repeated these same movements two times, four times, according to the time of day. At night, jackals prowled around, but each time they got close, my prayers held off the perspective of their feast.

After three days of total fasting, my limbs had stiffened. Suffering gradually took over my entire body, like quicksand. My lips, mouth, and throat dried out and cracked. My stomach and intestines tightened up and were twisted slowly by a prodigious force, as if it were wringing the last drops of liquid from them. A raging fire burned my entrails, the blaze then spreading up to my face, hands, and chest. I felt profound fear, dreadful anguish and a ferocious hatred of the human species. For hours, atrocious pain radiated throughout my nerves and muscles, getting worse in sudden bursts, followed by slow lulls. A powerful vice painfully compressed my head and brain, and violent fits of fever racked my body, beginning with severe shivering, then despondency, then gradual euphoria. The pain eased up, the spasms stopped, and my legs stretched out. My panting, exhausted flesh no longer needed anything—no longer felt hunger or thirst. I heard buzzing sounds—impressions of chloroform through long sound waves. I now felt infinite presences around me, a chorus of friendly voices. The entire desert was full of people watching me die. The vultures approached me and put their rough feet with sharp claws on my body. When they struck me with their powerful beaks, my body shook in a violent and desperate convulsion. The vultures let go and leapt back, beating their huge, outstretched wings.

I was in a new world, where insignificant and bizarre memories of my departing life besieged me like the vultures that I chased away but who kept returning. A cottony cloud laden with rain had descended from the sky. It rested on my forehead, passing over my neck and chest before returning to my forehead. The moisture gradually revived the body and delirium gave way to sensations but sounds and shapes were still bathed in a blurry haze.

A green figure was clearly outlined in the air, standing out from the liquefied, obscure, and shapeless surroundings. The water was now in the entire organism, infiltrating through the pores, irrigating the organs, resuscitating the brain. The proud spirit was reborn from the water. I was stretched out on my back in the same place, on top of the cliff. The sun had woven its immobile web, flooding the sky and the earth with light. Once again, I looked at the blurry figure behind its green halo.

"Al-Khadir!"

"So, you have decided to change eras for a second time?"

"Al-Khadir! It's outrageous what's happening here! It's

148

a terrible era, full of injustice and evil people. Al-Nacrani has multiplied. Now there are hundreds of them in charge of armies of soldiers and their followers who come from everywhere to conquer us. They want to enslave the entire country. Even the masters have become slaves! I want no more of this era—I can no longer bear it! I want to live elsewhere or die!"

"Then once again go far into the future! Keep running after your chimera and change eras for the last time! But you will not be able to leave the next stop—you will stay there until you die!"

And he faded rapidly away, along with his green halo.

Imdel

I opened my eyes and closed them again immediately, blinded by the sun. I sat up and looked all around. I was there, on top of an ocher cliff, with no knowledge of who I was or why I was there. I was neither hungry nor thirsty and had no plans. I started to descend this imposing rocky barrier, dark with colors ranging from blackish to purplish-blue, breaking up the monotony of sand extending as far as the eye could see to the north as well as to the south. I was soon among the dunes. I wandered aimlessly, from slope to crumbling slope, and on to the next crumbling slope, buffeted between the crests and hollows of these enormous swells, without encountering the least sign of life. Yet not a single detail escaped me—I could see the smallest grain of sand in all its facets. And then there appeared the first sign of life: a meager broom shrub with roots laid bare by the driving wind and, upon one of its branches, a robber fly, or rather, a monster!

What catastrophe, what aberrant mutation could have caused this insect's head to become so disproportionate, its monstrous third eye to form, its proboscis to grow so long?

Its antennae—normally reddish-brown—had become a glossy black. It had lost all the claws on its legs, and its thorax had turned to metallic green. Its ivory-white legs were wrapped tightly around the miraculously green branch. It tried to fly off by spreading its glassy, highly iridescent wings lined with yellowish veins—but its disproportionately large head, covered in a silvery-gray pruinosity, made these efforts ridiculously pointless. Its three antero-internal compound eyes dilated. Tossed about violently by the vagaries of the wind, the little clump of broom shrub—whose roots were already partially exposed—was perched upon the fragile bundle of its few roots that were still anchored in the shifting ground. Each gust of wind might uproot the shrub and fling the robber fly far up into the air in the middle of a corrosive cloud of white and gold sand grains, thereby saving it the arduous effort of having to fly by itself. But the young shrub still clung to its perch, with a ring of sand still packed in around its dried-out roots that were no more than a spindly fibrous tract. The swaying movement accelerated, forcing certain roots to bend over into an arch, while others— stretched to their limit—took over the normal functions of the root and the mechanical role of anchoring. A violent gust of wind caused the downwind arches to give way and the tuft violently struck the ground. The robber fly, stunned, had not been thrown off its branch. The broom shrub was now attached to the sand by only a few uphill roots, and then by one single long root, curiously reminiscent of the mooring line of a ship at anchor.

Unable to fly, the robber fly had folded its useless

wings and pressed its glossy black abdomen against the stem of the branch. At the end of its mooring, the tuft was still waving back and forth in the wind, recording the directional variations of the wind in the sand like a seismograph, until—violently torn up for good—its mooring line snapped and it was swept away by the wind, taking the robber fly with it in a whirlwind. I looked up, my eyes following the tuft's wild race through the quivering *barkhan* dunes and saw a wall of barbed wire at the base of a tall, very light brown fixed dune. I walked toward it.

Emerging from the sand at the base of the dune, hugging its steep slope, reaching far above its summit and stretching all along it to the left as well as to the right, as far as the eye could see, a gigantic wall of barbed wire cut off the horizon like a vision of the end of the world. Signs were embedded into the metal wall at regular intervals, like terrible threats: a dead man's head over two tibia bones in black on a white background; a flame above a black circle on a yellow background; a black flame with seven red vertical lines on a white background; three crescents on a circle with an inscription below it in black on a white background; a black clover and an inscription followed by a red vertical bar on a white background; a black clover on a yellow background with a word followed by two vertical red lines on a white background and an inscription; a black clover on a yellow background with an inscription followed by three vertical red lines and another inscription on a white background. The entire surface of the ferrous wall was decorated with medals of this type.

At the top of the dune, a sentinel paced back and forth

on an interminable patrol, walking slowly and kicking up sand with each step of their heavy boots. The sentinel wore protective glasses and a mask under a helmet. Gloved hands held a combat gun furnished with a bayonet. Other sentinels were visible, at regular intervals, all along the ridge of the dune, too high and too regular to be the work of the natural forces of the desert. Upon the slope, human skeletons were scattered here and there. I felt a sharp thump against my temple that instantly radiated throughout my brain, and I collapsed face-first onto the sand.

When I woke up, I was tied to a chair in an empty room. I must have been at some height because I saw below me, through the closed window in front of me, lines of dunes overlooking a completely flat and empty pit. Then I distinguished immense hangars that seemed to be carved into the sand in the depression, camouflaged by their exactly matching color. A wide black strip ran down the slope and branched out into the depression. It was being used by red ants smeared with florescent inscriptions. Two strangely dressed men came into the room, speaking and gesturing to me in a threatening manner. I didn't understand anything they were saying. They started to hit me violently and sent me rolling across the floor with the chair. Then they made me swallow some huge, salty-tasting capsules that nearly choked me and left me in a half-conscious daze.

The gigantic ants were still swarming about even after night fell. Now, in the powerful light of projectors, their eyes were illuminated. I was able to sleep that night, and I dreamed that I was a time traveler, descending from the top of the mountain in search of a better humanity. I knew that it was my last chance, that my search ended here, that it was here I must die my veritable death, in accordance with the pact I had made with al-Khadir. I came across the gigantic wall of barbed wire cutting off the horizon, like a vision of the end of the world. I saw the fennec fox come along to steal "for fun." I saw it successfully pull off the impossible feat of getting past that infernal metal wall. But its ubiquity and nocturnal audacity were crushed when it discovered the giant ants, and it came back out very soon, empty-handed. Usually so resourceful, it knew that it could never steal something here! The fennec fox was never quite the same after it came out—sometimes it thought it was a jerboa, and sometimes it thought it was a desert crow. It had the lingering and unpleasant impression that its tail was going to get ahead of it as it ran!

One day, they came and got me at dawn. Low ocher-colored buildings were arranged along the gentle slope of the cliff, in between piles of huge fallen blocks still flooded with the yellow light of the powerful projectors. A giant portrait was displayed on a sign posted in the center of the circular intersection. The dark face exuded ferocity. The whites of the eyes sunken behind overly prominent eyebrows were brilliant, like those uranium-based false teeth. The flat nose with enormous nostrils was turned up, preventing the thick lips from touching each other, making his expression stuck in a perpetual hideous smile. Below the portrait was an inscription that I could not decipher.

They put me in another cell whose walls were strewn with thick, dark, built-in mirrors that were speaking and displaying images. I later understood that they were teaching me their language. I remained there for days, weeks, or months—I never knew, since the absence of clocks, visitors, and regular meals caused me to lose my sense of time in there. Once, in a dream, I saw again the gigantic portrait in the middle of the circular intersection, and I recognized him as my descendant. I always recognized my descendants when I met them, thanks to their looks, but it was always in a dream, after the fact, like now, when I recovered my consciousness as a time traveler. In the preceding era, I had recognized them at various ages— some were children, adults or old people. They were in the most diverse situations—civilian and military, rich and poor, masters and slaves, good and bad, beautiful and ugly, black and mixed-race. They all had that same expression in their eyes that never fooled me and allowed me to identify them every time. Whenever I recognized one, I made the firm decision to speak to him as soon as I woke up, to give him a sign, to warn him. But when I woke up, I had already forgotten my dreams and my identity—I had lost my consciousness as a traveler through time, and no one meant anything in particular to me anymore. I found myself completely disconnected from my dreams and my past. Even this awareness of my inability, of the rupture between waking and sleeping, was but a dream—a ghost visiting my sleep. Awake, I was there, a simple shape dressed up, fitted out, and cut off from everything else— other beings were completely foreign to me.

When I left my cell, I knew a lot about that cursed language that was starting to drive me crazy. The truck taking me away passed through the intersection, and this time I could decipher the inscription below the portrait: "His Excellency Tangalla Ould Matalla, President of the Democratic Republic of Barzakh." I was transferred to another cell with a fellow prisoner who was in worse shape and more depressed than I was. They kept showing us the same video program, so I asked why they were force-feeding us so many useless images and words. He told me that we would be forced to join the teams and work along with them and would stay in these warehouses for the rest of our lives! The video kept hammering away. The program was on an infinite loop, repeating the same soundtrack over and over again:

"...Imdel, one of the facilities for storing toxic waste and hazardous materials in the Democratic Republic of Barzakh. All these facilities are built in the Great Desert. This vast territory is a universe of sand made up of very diverse landscapes—shifting, crisscrossing dunes that are difficult to access, separated and nonlinear; depressions of sand-free piedmont that separate the escarpments from the dune massifs; tablelands and escarpments; shallow valleys; plateaus isolated by erosion and crowned by a table of hard limestone or sandstone rock; zones of expansion carpeted in alluvium made up of clayey sand; cone-shaped inselbergs; depressions between dunes in the form of funnels; narrow gorges and transverse valleys; little hillocks of sand forming arrows in the wind, behind shrubs or behind rocky buttes, which serve as markers of various importance. Vast regs covered in pebbles or a fine dusting of sand that, in the sunset, joins the sky to the earth; rocky promontories and sandy corridors through towering dunes.

"This region, one of the most arid on the planet, is a magical place, but cruel for humans. Extremely high temperatures have been recorded here, and starting at the beginning of April, it can regularly reach temperatures of 190 degrees at ground level in the middle of the day. The winds are always full of sand and blow perpetually no matter the season— the most famous of these winds is the Harmattan, the Saharan wind that activates the ripening of dates in July. The only plants or animals that can survive in this harsh world are those who, for generation upon generation, over thousands of years, have managed to adapt to this cruel environment. The ungulate best suited to life in the desert was the beautiful addax antelope, which lived and thrived in the sandy immensity of the Great Desert, where a tribe, that of the N'madis—desert hunters— established itself thanks to the dog hunting of antelopes. Due to the foresight of our dearly beloved President, His Excellency Tangalla Ould Matalla, we were able to turn this previously useless area into profitable land. Storage Facilities for Toxic Waste and Hazardous Materials now operate here for the greater good of the international community, creating a significant source of income for our country.

"The construction and operation of these facilities strictly adhere to international safety standards. The solidly built warehouses have iron bars on all the windows. The exterior walls are steel-coated, while the internal dividing walls— designed to prevent fires from spreading and extending above the ceiling by approximately one meter— are reinforced with pilasters and remain independent from the adjacent structure to prevent collapse in the event of a fire. The pipes and electrical cables running through them are placed in fire-retardant sand shells. The fire doors close automatically in the event of a fire, thanks to melt-away joints activated by the flames. The cable connected to the melt-away joints passes through the counterweight ring, and the inclined track ensures the automatic closure of the doors, including emergency exits equally resistant to fire.

"The pictograms—red on a white background, white, yellow, and red on a blue background, white on blue, and black on white—specify that smoking is not allowed, and indicate the location of emergency equipment, telephones, and emergency exits. Safety rules are posted. Emergency exits are clearly marked as such and positioned in accordance with basic safety regulations, to facilitate an orderly exit in case of emergency. They are designed to be opened easily in the dark or in dense smoke and equipped with crash bars. They provide escape routes from the warehouse in three directions. Access to the exits is marked by black lines and arrows on a yellow background, and exits are protected by poles painted in these same colors, so they will not be blocked.

"The waterproof floors are smooth without being slippery and have no cracks, which makes them easy to clean. They are surrounded by raised ledges to contain leaks and contaminated water, used to control fires. Inclined planes whose slopes do not exceed 1 in 50 are built across exterior access points, with the edge of the inclined plane located outside the warehouse. Additional low walls are placed on each side of the inclined plane to ensure complete retention of liquids. When open, the ventilation panels fitted to the roofs represent 3% of the surface area of the floor. They open automatically in the event of a fire to let smoke and heat escape, thereby aiding in locating the source of the fire and slowing its spread.

"The waste materials and hazardous products stored in the open-air mines are carefully selected for their exposure to high temperatures that might lead to thermal degradation. To avoid contamination of the water table, the flooring of the storage area has been coated with a waterproof and heat-resistant layer. The containers are stacked and stored vertically on pallets.

"When products arrive at the Facility, they are identified by their labels and bill of lading. The supplier submits safety data records. The quantity and condition of the products are then verified based on the information received. The conveyor presents the transport document which lists the name, address, and telephone number of the transport company, the name of the product to be transported, the principal risks, the precautions to be taken, and instructions in case of accident or leakage.

"The storage itself follows a stocking plan based on the nature of the products to store. An empty space is always maintained between the exterior walls and the merchandise closest to the edge as well as in between the stacks, to ensure ventilation and allow easy access for inspectors and firefighters. The products are arranged so that forklifts and other pieces of loading equipment, or emergency vehicles, can move around freely. The aisles and corners are wide enough to minimize any risk of deterioration of the stored merchandise. The aisles, passageways, and paths reserved for forklifts are marked on the floor, and foot traffic is not allowed in these areas in order to prevent obstructions or bodily harm. The height of the stacks never exceeds three meters.

"This plan, posted at the entrance of each warehouse, clearly states the risks associated with each section, indicating the subsection number of each distinct cell, the location and quantity of the stored products or groups of products and the risks they present, the location of emergency and fire-fighting material, access points, and emergency exits. You will notice at the bottom of the plan, in large red letters, that it is expressly forbidden for staff to eat, drink, or smoke in the work zones.

"Now, you see the rocky zone on the opposite side that extends across a wide band of several kilometers—this is the most radioactive area. Deep wells have been drilled out as landfills for vitrified radioactive waste. You might notice that, in places, the rocks have developed cracks due to the powerful heat sources contained within them, but these fractures are regularly sealed up.

"When leaving the storage zone, the employees must go through the decontamination changing rooms before taking the sky tram to the dorms. Work clothing and special personal protection equipment are decontaminated and left in the changing rooms until the next work shift."

The men coming out of the changing rooms to take the sky tram no longer even remotely resembled the sinister creatures who had gone in. Masks, gloves, and boots were gone. The heavy white suits had given way to ample blue boubous in richly embroidered cotton. Their exposed faces expressed a thousand nuanced sorrows of the human species. Their complexion, made pale by their masks, retained its coppery color in spite of everything. Many had the drawn and wrinkled features so often found in cancer ward patients. Their eyes expressed their resignation to suffering and death.

"...Failure to follow the safety rules and regulations will be severely punished!"

"What?"

"What's your name?" the other guy repeated.

"I don't know... Maybe I never had a name, or maybe I did have one, but if so, I must have forgotten it."

"Well, now! You're a strange one! You don't have a name... and where do you come from?"

"I don't know..."

"Are you messing with me, or what?"

"No, I mean it! The me that you see, a normal guy who

looks much older than you—I do not know who I am or where I come from! All that I know about myself is that I opened my eyes not very long ago for what really seemed to me to be the very first time. I looked around myself and saw that I was at the top of a cliff. I didn't know who I was or why I was there. So, I walked down into the dunes and was wandering around aimlessly when I bumped into the barbed wire around the Facility."

On the screens, the program had started up again for the umpteenth time: "...Imdel, one of the facilities for storing toxic waste and hazardous materials in the Democratic Republic of Barzakh..."

"Do you believe me?"

"No! I can't believe such a story! Either you're sick or you have amnesia!"

"And what about you—who are you? Why are you here?"

"I come from Windcity, the capital. They sentenced me to forced labor. I was accused of sympathizing with the ecologists and passing information to 'Save the Sahara.' But what they really resent is the fact that I'm N'madi."

"N'madi?"

"Yeah, the N'madis who used to hunt addax—they talk about us in the program. We used to be masters of the Great Desert and lived free in these great magical spaces. We rejected technology and the world of technology in order to protect our space. But, when Tangalla came to power, he signed an agreement with the United Nations and our territory was classified as an international storage zone for toxic waste and hazardous products. We were all deported to the coast or to other regions of the country. A long time ago our territory was transformed into an international trash bin. I was born in Windcity, long after the deportation. Today, the Earth is classified as an international dump and almost everyone who used to live here emigrated long ago to other planets. No one still lives on Earth except the outcasts of the solar system who are abandoned to the effects of pollution and radioactivity. Every chance they get, they send us to forced labor in the SFTWHP where no one ever survives for more than two years!"

"But that's horrible! So, we're going to die here?"

"Once in a while, 'Save the Sahara' sets off a bomb in one of the facilities or kills the drivers of an isolated truck. But all that is but a drop in the bucket—it doesn't stop Tangalla from opening up a new facility every three months!"

The Era of Tangalla

That night I slept fitfully and when I entered the dreaming phase, I recovered my past identity and consciousness. And I began to cry out, calling with all my might for the Green One,

'Al-Khadir! Al-Khadir! What mess have you gotten me into? Let me out of here! You know perfectly well that I'm traveling through time in search of a better humanity—but this one is the worst of all! Don't leave me here!'

My tears, cries, and supplications finally worked and he consented to appear, still just as hazy behind his green halo.

'Gara, have you forgotten our pact?'

'No, I remember everything!'

'Then you should remember that I gave you the power to travel to the future because you wanted to change eras...'

'Yes, I thought that men were evolving towards something better!'

'So, you chose to explore the future. I allowed you to explore one or two eras, as you wished, since you didn't want to live in the time of Awdaghost any longer. You used your power for the first time and found yourself nine centuries later. And since there was no possibility

for you to return to the past, you had to either stay in that era or use the power I entrusted to you one last time, with the risk of finding yourself in an even worse era and this time having to stay there definitively. That was what we agreed upon. But in spite of all that, you decided to leave that era and you used, for the last time, the power I entrusted to you, and found yourself in the era of Tangalla. And now you want to leave again! You will never travel through time again—you will die here!'

'I want to go back and leave this accursed era! I have never seen evil this close!'

'There is no longer any way back. What man before you has had the chance to live his life between three different eras that are so far removed from each other? You're only getting what you deserve with your ignorance and pride. You cannot forever want to escape your destiny—you are condemned to live in your era and accept it. Anyway, this era represents the ultimate face of the Earth. If you had gone even further, you would have found the Earth reduced to a pile of burnt ashes!' And he faded away gradually along with his green halo.

'No! Wait! Wait! Al-Khadir! Al-Khadir!'

When I awoke, I was shaking and my head was as heavy as if it were made of lead. My tongue felt cottony, and my throat felt sticky. The N'madi was holding my hand.

"What's wrong with you? Who was that person you were calling?"

"Give me something to drink."

He asked again, "Who was that person you were call-ing?"

"I was calling someone? When?"

"Just now—you woke me up, crying out 'Al-Khadir!' 'Khadir,' or something like that."

"Huh, that's strange. I don't remember anything!"

"You worry me! I'm going to keep an eye on you!"

The next day, someone came to get us at dawn. He was armed and hollering, threatening us with the worst possible abuses. Before leading us out, he said, "I'm taking you to the changing rooms where you will get ready for work! You are now on the day team. You are assigned to the mining zone. So, move it!"

We were among the first to arrive at the changing rooms. He showed us two metal lockers for our clothes and made us take ice-cold showers that smelled awful and made my skin sting. Then we were given heavy, slick white suits to put on and heavy boots, masks, and gloves to wear. Then we waited, hunched over on a narrow bench. The employees moved around like sleepwalkers, and no one spoke. Some seemed to be suffering dreadfully but remained silent. Then everyone was given two huge bitter pills that we swallowed as quickly as we could.

The sun was already glaring down from the top of the cliff when the sky tram dropped us off. There were three of us in the mining zone, which was situated in the rocky region on the opposite side. The foreman made us inspect all the wells to locate the cracks that had appeared since the day before.

"Here is how we're going to proceed," he said. "You two, are going to collect the stone blocks from the slope over there, and I mean the big blocks, not the little rocks, and you're going to put them in the grinder. I will drive the machine and I will position the deck to pour the molten rock into the cracks. Let's go! Get a move on, you lazy bums! I've got my eye on you!"

By the end of the afternoon, when the shadows cast by our suits had already climbed up the slope of the cliff, an alarm sounded from all directions, signaling the end of the work-day. In the changing room, when I had taken off my suit, I poked myself gingerly, surprised to find that my body was still solid. They took us back to the dorms.

The staff dormitories were constructed on one of highest peaks of the cliff—a group of low prefab houses accessible by one of the sky trams. This summit overlooked the *baten* with huge shiny square blocks on its jagged, uneven ledge shot through with a dense network of joints and breaks, giving the landscape a chaotic look. I was shown to my place in the bunk room—a cot placed next to a metal locker, like the ones in the changing room. I collapsed onto the bed and remained unconscious for a moment. I jumped up when I heard a siren. I thought it was in my head, but I saw the others head toward the door. I followed them down a long hallway leading to an open door with tall panels attached to rails. Above it, a glowing inscription indicated the purpose of the place and, to the right, in front of the double doors, there was a small blackboard with writing in yellow chalk: "Menu. Wednesday, December 20/2045. Potassium soup. Steak and fried mushrooms. Dates from Aghreijit."

I took my place on a bench in the middle of the others. Two neat and tidy servers went around to all the tables. One pushed a cart with steaming containers while the other served up soup with a long ladle. The guy sitting next to me started to scream like a madman, took his full plate, and threw it up into the face of the server who was pushing the cart. Security came and took him away, beating him soundly while everyone else continued as if nothing happened.

As we left the cafeteria, security came to get both the N'madi and myself and took us to the office of the Administrator. They made us wait there for half an hour. We sat there on chairs, just waiting outside his door, not knowing what he wanted from us. The two security guards at the door were chatting away and seemed to ignore us, but the big unrestrained dog resting at our feet kept his eyes on us and growled at our every move. When the buzzer above the door sounded, one of the security officers ushered us in.

A short, remarkably plump man wearing khaki shorts and a short-sleeved shirt had his back to us. He was standing between the desk and the long table holding computer monitors and keyboards. His head was closely shaven and rolls of fat on the back of his neck rose all the way up to the back of his head. You could see the arms of his glasses lodged in the flesh behind his ears. The door to the office had already been closed behind us, but the Administrator still had his back to us, fiddling with his keyboards. Then he turned around and looked at us over the top of his glasses. His low forehead was creased and there were almost no eyebrows above his sunken light-brown eyes, which held the same expression as the computer screen he had just left. His thin pursed lips and exposed double chin were evidence of his bureaucratic worries. He had reddish spots on his face and lots of pimples on his neck and chest. His stomach protruded out between the buttons of his too-short shirt and his knees were drowning in the flesh from his thighs. His bare feet were in plastic sandals. He went behind the desk, collapsed into his chair and waved his hand at us.

"Sit down," he said, handing us some printouts. "Read these before signing them. They're your work and lodging contracts. You may well be convicts, but you have your rights guaranteed by our Constitution!"

"Convicts?" I protested. "But I was never on trial or convicted by anyone!"

"*You* are a special case—you were caught red-handed."

"Red-handed? But what do they accuse me of? What did I do to be a prisoner here?"

"You tried to sabotage the Facility—you were found lurking around the border!"

"I swear to you I was only there by accident!"

"I don't give a damn! You're wasting my time! I don't want to hear about it! To me, you're a prisoner just like all the others. After all, they can't sentence you without knowing who you are and what your motives are. The ongoing investigation will decide that. We've sent your description out to all the police since we couldn't get anything out of you. In the meantime, you're a prisoner here!"

The N'madi watched us in disillusioned silence—he had already signed his print-out without reading it.

"I won't sign anything!" I said with feigned confidence. "I was not convicted so I have nothing to sign!"

The buzzer sounded, the door opened, and the security guards came into the office.

"Take the N'madi back to the dorms and throw this guy into the persuasion room!"

One of the men grabbed me roughly by the arm and, in spite of my protests, locked me in an empty room with glass eyes covering the walls. After a moment, I found myself in pitch darkness. Then beams of multicolored light converged on me from every direction, compressing my brain. I felt a horrific pain in my head. A few moments later, the beams faded away and light returned to the room. The man who had locked me in opened the door and I was again taken to the Administrator who casually handed me the print-out.

"Sign here," he said, pointing to the bottom of the page. I signed where he told me to.

"Take him back now!"

The lights were on back at the dorm, but I saw no one. I looked around everywhere, curious that no one was there.

"They've left," said a voice behind me, near the door. "They're always at the club at this time of night."

I turned around and saw someone who was half-standing, legs spread apart, bent so far over that his head grazed the ground and his arms stretched out behind him between his legs. He straightened up only to fold over backwards, arching his back, dropping his head, and placing both hands on the ground, behind his heels. I asked what he was doing there.

"I'm doing my daily calisthenics—one hour every night, before going to bed. It rounds out my hour of jogging in the mornings—nothing like it to stay healthy and maintain the body's equilibrium."

"Healthy? And a balanced body? Here!"

He launched into a long explanation that I could not follow because of my headache. He was still talking long after I had gone to bed.

"You know, as long as there is life…."

The moment I was asleep, I regained my consciousness as a time traveler.

So, I have really gone to another era! Ten centuries, according to the date on that chalkboard menu! And to end up in a place like this!

Solima

Every night, I invoked Al-Khadir while I slept, but in vain. Once, in my dream, Vala Awdaghostia visited me but as a N'madia woman. She helped me out of the Facility and took me on a crazy race across the Great Desert, hunting phantom addaxes. I was out of breath from running after her; I wanted desperately to catch up and speak to her. When one of her dogs had taken down a phantom addax and she had stopped to look at it, I was finally able to rejoin her, and, taking her in my arms, I confessed my despair to her.

'Vala, my darling! What misfortune, what a curse! Vala! Vala! Tangalla is our descendant!'

'Tangalla? Who is Tangalla?'

'The monster, of course—the polluter, the President of Barzakh!'

'Who told you that? How do you know?'

'I know! I know! He's our descendant. I recognize them all! They all have that same expression in their eyes that lets me recognize them every time! If I had known, I would not have fallen in love with you in Awdaghost!'

But she had already taken off after her dogs, in pursuit of another phantom prey.

In the morning, before dawn, we were in the mining zone.
Every night the radioactive substances buried deep beneath
the rocks caused new fissures, and we rolled more stones
over to be fed into the melting machine that sealed the
cracks with molten rock. When I arrived that morning, I
glanced downhill. Thin clouds of quartz sand coming off
the top of the crescent dunes made them look like they were
smoking. The wind was going to pick up. Further down near
the bottom of the depression, the big red carriers swarmed
in every direction, and white suits shuttled between the
warehouses and the trucks parked out front. The drilling
machine was in our zone—it was digging a deep well into
the rock. The foreman wouldn't let us gather up the loose
rocks; instead, he made us go get the stone blocks further
uphill, in the rockslide area.

One day, the Administrator summoned me and handed me
an envelope.

"Here's your allowance," he said with no other
explanation.

That night, I was able to go to the club for the first
time. After eating in the cafeteria, I went with the N'madi
and some other prisoners. We took the elevator down to the
basement. We all squeezed in together so we could arrive at
the same time. It was suffocating and smelled abominably,
and I coughed to drive off the thought of fainting. When the

elevator finally opened up, we found ourselves in a hallway entirely covered in mirrors. Some of them shamelessly took advantage of this to adjust their clothing and smooth their hair. Others dared not look their misery in the face. I glimpsed a head of graying hair that seemed to be mine. Then a door opened up and we started down a long, dimly lit hallway. At the far end, we got in line behind an automatic ticket machine. Each of us put his money into the machine and got a coupon in exchange. Then we entered one by one by inserting our coupon into the little slot on the right marked with a red arrow, which opened the door long enough for one person to go in at a time and then closed again.

When I went in, I hesitated for a moment, undecided, not knowing which direction to go. The deafening music passed right over my ears and penetrated directly into every part of my body, the bass notes pounding my heart like a resounding bell. The steamy mixture of stale alcohol, tobacco, sweat, and damp furniture gave the stagnant air its characteristic odor, exiling oxygen to a faraway place, nothing more than a memory. Red and blue lamps disseminated a conspiratorial half-light. Way out in front, a deluge of multicolored spotlights made rainbows over a raised square thronged with writhing, indistinct bodies. Off to the right, crystal glasses were set out on the golden counter of a huge semi-circular bar, where several silhouettes perched on high stools. I felt someone take me by the hand.

"Are you new? Still shy? Come on, my little desert fox, let's find a place to sit!"

I followed her without thinking and didn't have time to

distinguish the traits of her face. Her thick black hair tumbled across her shoulders and hid her elusive profile from me. She had me sit on a deep couch pushed up next to a low table, and, just before heading up toward the bar, she murmured something into my ear, but I couldn't understand it because it was drowned out by the sound of the music. I had time to look at her more carefully when she came back and placed two full glasses on the table, plopping down heavily on the couch in front of me.

"Excuse me," she said, slightly embarrassed. "I must have gained weight here."

"I dare not ask your name since I don't know mine."

"It's no big deal. My name here is Solima."

The makeup on her face was not heavy and her full lips were not devoid of sensuality. But, above her delicate nose, her huge moist eyes expressed an unfathomable sadness. They were like beaches upon which every wave of hope comes to be broken. As she moved her arm forward to take her glass, I saw on her right wrist a strange bracelet that had a dial with a fixed arrow in the middle, immersed in a transparent liquid. I was sickened by the music—a decidedly anonymous rhythm section playing a perverse refrain that obediently evoked human stupidity. The instrumental arrangement was overbearing and smothered the melody. A hopelessly monotone voice was stuck in one octave, spouting absurd little anecdotes, sung in the first person, constructed in short, very simple verses. It was nothing but a useless clatter of smarmy songs, poorly written and drowning in complacency.

"I hate the music here!" she said suddenly. "What about you? You don't seem to like it!"

Her comment took me by surprise. Could we have similar tastes? Or could it be nothing more than a manifestation of the old feminine instinct that prompts women to show themselves to men as mere empty masks, phantoms with no souls under their clothing and jewelry, an exact copy of the male who approaches them, a simple mirror for his dreams and his desires?

"You're not going to answer me?" she asked impatiently, taking hold of my hand in her eagerness.

"Yes, of course… I hate this clatter of useless noise that obediently evokes human stupidity!"

I noticed that my words delighted her and caused her great pleasure, as if she was drinking them right out of my mouth. Inexplicably, I felt a shiver run up and down my body.

"Let's leave, if you want to!" she said. "We can go to a different room in the club. Hey, why not go to the billiards room?"

In the billiards room, no one's mind was on the game. A man with a disproportionately large head was standing on top of the table. His eyes were shining like those of a visionary consumed with feverish passion. His thick, scraggly black beard came down to his chest, and he wore a little white embroidered cap and waved his hands around as he spoke. People were crowding around him—some yanking on his clothes and threatening him, others laughing and mocking him, calling out insults. A few others seemed to be listening to him attentively, trying to grasp the meaning of his words. The shouting of the crowd around the table prevented me from hearing what he was saying. Then someone yelled:

"Shut up already! Let him speak!"

The din abated slightly, and I could hear what he was saying:

"...the Occultation Cycle. God has removed his proof from this earth where corruption and evil reign. But the day is near when the Iman of this era, the Mahdi, will come to destroy the evil and restore the just..."

"We don't need your Mahdi," someone called out. "The wheel of destiny has crushed us so completely that we no longer expect anything from Heaven!"

"Yeah," someone else added. "If any hope of salvation remains, it'll come from this goddamn Earth!"

"Anyway, *we* can't afford the luxury of waiting any longer!"

"And what makes you think this guy of yours will ever come?"

"And when? Huh?"

"I swear to you that he will come! He spoke to me—I saw him in a dream... Yes, I swear! He only appears to his faithful believers... He told me, 'For a long time now, this Earth has given in to corruption and evil, and now the time of the just will begin!'"

"All right, that's enough! We've heard your rant, now get down! Let's get back to playing!"

"And when did he say he'd come, your messiah?"

"When the current cycle ends..."

"Oh, right! When the Earth is already burnt up, engulfed by the Sun!"

"Sure, but can you be more precise?"

"I don't know… In fifty years… maybe a hundred…"

At this point, a burst of shrill, impertinent laughter could be heard from the back of the room, causing everyone to turn around. It came from a lone woman, standing with her back against the wall.

"Yes, I'm telling you!" insisted the visionary. "We are at the end of the twelfth Occultation Cycle, which is the last one! The cycle of time will start again, opening with a cycle of Truth Manifested, and this cycle will begin with the arrival of the Mahdi…"

He was interrupted by the arrival of the Administrator, along with a dozen security guards wearing metal helmets and brandishing their clubs.

"All right, you there! Get down! Get him down! Come on now, move out of the way!"

"You are soldiers of Evil! The corrupt of the Earth!" cried the visionary as he fought back.

"You can think whatever you want," the Administrator said to the visionary. "You can say whatever you want; we are a democracy, after all! Just never disturb the public order, or you'll have to deal with me! Go on, take him! Throw his ass into the persuasion room for the night!"

Then, before leaving the room, he said to the others, "Think about it. You can say whatever you want, you can lie, scheme and cheat, but do not disturb the peace! Ever!"

When he had left, billiard games started up again and conversations became hushed.

"Do you want to play a game?" she asked in a lively voice.

"No, I've never played this game."

"Then let's go sit down!"

We sat at a table next to the woman who had laughed so impertinently. I was more and more intrigued by her bracelet.

"Your bracelet is pretty," I said, caressing its jewel.

"It's not a bracelet, it's my compass. It points me toward just souls. You are the first good man I've met here on Earth!"

"What did you say?"

She lifted her bracelet toward my face.

"It's our hunting tool," she said. "I'm part of a tribe of intergalactic hunters in search of souls of justice. We live off conversations with just souls. I live, breathe, and am nourished by this type of conversation, which for me is just as vital as oxygen, water, and food are to you. I am like those beings who wander the night that you call 'vampires,' except the blood I need are the words that come out of your mouth. For thousands of your years, I have been traveling across a black hole and all over the Milky Way, but just souls are so rare..."

"Thousands of years! But you look barely thirty!"

"I am like those images from the past you see in your sky that you call 'stars'—some took hundreds of billions of years to get here, their voyage having started long ago, sometimes even before the birth of your galaxy. I'll give you an example—see that woman sitting just three meters from us at the other table? I don't see her as she is now, but rather as she was a hundredth of a millionth of a second ago, or a hundredth of a microsecond. Of course, you can't tell the difference on such a minute time scale, but imagine what that means on the cosmic scale... the last just soul I met was an exile from Vega in retirement on Phobos... Then, since I planned to take off in search of some just souls on Earth, I spent some time in Libya, at point 32 of the Earth map of Mars. There's an Earth Studies Center there where I stayed for six Martian years, or a little less than twelve of your years, in order to study the civilizations and languages of Earth and shift myself into a shape that would resemble an earthling. You have no idea what an effort that is— it's like being recreated a second time! I always do those preparations and that preliminary shape shift every time I want to communicate with a being from a new civilization. Now, tell me about yourself—say something!"

I told her everything I knew about myself, ever since that day on the clifftop, when I opened my eyes into the blinding sun for the first time, up until my arrival at the club that evening. It seemed to me that she knew more about me than I knew about myself. I asked her to lend me her bracelet, telling her that her compass would be really useful since most of the brief lives that blink upon the surface of this ball of silicate and iron have long since lost their sense of direction! But she explained to me that her compass was powered by her life energy and wouldn't work for a human.

When they announced that the club was going to close, I told her that I would love to see her again the next night, but she made excuses, launching into a lengthy explanation filled with nostalgia and sadness.

"I have crossed so many galactic deserts in search of you, but I must leave. I cannot drink from the same source more than once... You see, it's as if you were traveling across an immense desert towards a faraway destination on a set timetable. When you find a wellspring, you stop to drink, but you move on. You cannot stay at a single wellspring for it will eventually dry up. Earthly souls are fleeting like desert wellsprings! Yes, I must leave. This evening with you has aged me by several hundred years—you have no idea! I am forced to leave you in search of new blood, a new wellspring, another soul of justice. But if you suffer too much here, I can help you get out."

"What! Of course, I want to get out of this place!"

"I am going to give you one of my suits. When you put it on, you will be invisible and can leave whenever you want. My clothes—not the ones I wear for the club at the moment, but my usual clothes, are coveralls with integrated helmet, gloves and boots. These are invisibility cloaks, cut from a special fabric made up with reflective nano-antennas which scatter light waves so that the wearer becomes completely invisible from all angles. They are breathable, self-cleaning, and naturally antibacterial. They widen and shrink in all four directions to fit the size of the wearer."

I agreed to try out the suit, without really believing in its miraculous virtues.

"See you in a minute, in your dorm!" she told me before leaving.

I answered by telling her she was crazy and would get arrested by security.

"Don't worry about a thing, I'll wear my suit!"

We had just gotten into bed in the dorm with lights off when I felt an unfamiliar hand upon my body and heard Solima's voice in my ear. She came and snuggled up to me, pressed her mouth up against mine and begged me to say something. I murmured crazy words into her mouth—ravings that did not sound like my own, and that took my breath away.

When just before dawn she unstuck her mouth from mine, I was exhausted, annihilated, as if emptied of my own words. She said to me, in a changed voice:

"Goodbye, I hope to meet you again, in a different era, and drink from your wellspring a second time. I brought you the suit—it's under your bed."

I didn't answer her. I was incapable of saying or thinking anything—I had no more words! I felt my tongue and my brain emptied, dried out, splintered. I stayed in bed. The others had already finished eating and were getting ready to go to work. The N'madi came over and asked me if I was feeling sick. I gave no response, so he got worried and went to alert the Administrator who called for a doctor. The doctor diagnosed simple fatigue and prescribed a tonic and a day of rest. When the dormitory was empty, I took the suit from under the bed and locked it in my locker—you never know, the cleaning crew might suck it up with their vacuum cleaners. I stayed in my bed for the entire day, eyes open, doing nothing, thinking nothing. And that evening, when the N'madi returned from the mining zone, more miserable than Sisyphus, I still could not speak. Yet he found enough energy to lament my fate out loud.

"Poor guy! He had already lost his memories and now he loses his ability to speak too!"

I remained silent for several weeks, but that didn't stop the foreman from making me roll stones in the mining zone. Incidentally, upon closer examination, a mute Sisyphus might be worth more than a speaking one.

Vala N'madia

After a few months, no longer able to bear life in the Facility, I decided to search among my newly burgeoning speech for the
words needed to speak to the N'madi about my plan to escape. I didn't know where to go; the world for me was limited to the Facility. Perhaps there was nothing but facilities
like this everywhere. It was pointless to leave this one just to
end up in another one. I needed the N'madi's advice. At that
time, I was incapable of finding the word "suit" to explain to
him how I intended to escape. Without the word to describe
it, I tried to get him to touch it, but he stubbornly refused. I
insisted several times.

"Look! Touch! There! It's in my hands!"

But he wouldn't even deign to reach out his hand to
touch it, looking at me with bulging eyes and finally deciding
that I was crazy. After several days of discussing it through
gestures, punctuated with the occasional hesitant word, he
agreed to give me the address of Vala, a N'madia woman
who lived in Touil, the second station along the South highway as you left the Facility.

The next morning, I stayed in my bed waiting for everyone else to leave. When I was alone, I opened my locker and hastily put on Solima's suit. Then I crept out of the dormitory, dubious about Solima's nano-antennas, holding my breath and fearing that they would see me at every step. I avoided getting too close to the employees and security guards that I passed. I thought that, at any moment, they were going to turn around to face me and call me out. But I managed to make it to the sky tram and get in with the others without drawing any attention.

At the changing rooms, everyone got out to suit up for work and I stayed alone in the cabin with a security guard who was picking his nose with all ten fingers. I thought that he was going to notice my presence at any moment and shout threats at me, such as, "Hey, you there! What are you doing here? Why aren't you with the others? Get off!" But he continued to ignore me. The others got back in, totally hidden in their sinister suits, but still visible. And the sky tram continued its descent. I saw three men get off at the mining station, unable to tell which one was the N'madi, and then continued on to the loading zone. I got off and headed toward the closest truck, parked in front of one of the hangars. The two conveyors were filling out forms. I slipped through the cab door, which had been left open, and laid down on the bunk behind the seats. When they were done unloading, the two conveyors got back in, and the truck headed up to exit the Facility at the top of the cliff.

"I don't like Imdel," said the one who was driving. "The workers here are too complicated!"

"Yeah," said his partner, "the people here are so boring. I prefer the ones at the Aratane Facility who dance on their own graves!"

At the exit, the driver showed his pass and the huge gate topped in barbed wire opened to let the truck continue down the slope on the other side, toward the open sea of desert.

I was still just as worried. I told myself that the conveyors might find me, that they were going to notice my presence at my least movement on the bunk just behind them and as-sassinate me without any witnesses. However, I had to admit that Solima's nano-antennas had not betrayed me so far. Yet I was still worried. Maybe the truck had gone in the opposite direction from Touil. And if they were going in the right direction, were they going to stop at the Touil station? And if they stopped there, how was I going to get out without drawing their attention?

The codriver started to snore and the driver turned on the radio for a moment, tuning in to a remote station broadcasting news interspersed with music. Then, he put on automatic pilot, reclined his seat all the way back, almost crushing me, and indulged in watching a porn video. Later, when the codriver woke up, they launched into an interminable discussion about their plans.

"As for me," the codriver was saying, "I've saved up all my earnings for the past two years, but I'm not sure of the best way to turn them to profit. Sometimes I'm tempted to gamble, but it's too risky!"

"You can win big if you put your money in the races on Mars."

"No way! You don't know the bookies there!"

"You could try the stock market!"

"I'm not a big enough hitter—you need to have tons of money for that. No, I think I'll put my money in a savings account instead. Apparently, if you leave your money there for fifteen years without touching it, it will triple!"

"And what will you do with all that money in fifteen years?"

"I'll get married and build a cute little house, with an atomic bomb shelter!"

"Lucky dog! I'm not as lucky as you! I'm dead broke and yet my fiancée insists on getting married in five years, as soon as she finishes her bicycling trip around the Earth! I keep trying to get her to change her mind, but she's stubborn. You can't imagine how stubborn my fiancée is. I keep telling her over and over again that we can't get married in five years because we won't have enough money, but she doesn't want to hear it! Besides, it's not the money holding me back. Listen! Getting married means having kids, right?"

"Of course! Getting married means having kids and grandkids to dote upon in our old days, by the light of the fire in the evenings!"

"Yeah, but you see, I don't want to have kids! And my fiancée can't understand that. What's the point of having kids in a world as disgusting as this, in the middle of this international trash heap—kids who will be doomed to suffer and die wretched, surrounded by the pariahs of the solar system, with no possible way out?"

"You're such a pessimist! Maybe our kids and grandkids will find a way out of the dead-ends we've driven them into. But now that I think about it, maybe you are right after all. Our responsibility is too great. Well, shit! What a legacy!"

Toward the beginning of the afternoon, the truck slowed down and parked in a huge parking area in front of a building lit up with colorful flashing signs. Gigantic letters across the entire top of the front read, "TOUIL. Rest Stop. 24 Hours." The conveyors had gotten out and the driver was behind the open hood. The rumble of running motors filled the entire rest stop. Some trucks were parking while others were heading off toward the exit to get back onto the highway. The doors and hoods of the parked trucks stood open, with one or two men bustling about each one. I pushed the door open and jumped out, falling heavily on the asphalt. The driver lifted his head and looked in my direction, but eventually stuck his nose back in his engine. I left the truck without looking back.

The N'madi had told me that Vala's house was located behind the ditch to the right of the highway on the way out of Touil. He had even drawn out a basic map under the address. I fumbled for the piece of paper in the pocket of my suit but was having trouble finding it and grabbing on to it with my gloved hand. Then I saw in front of me, on the side of the highway, a signboard that read "Touil" with a red slash through it marking the limit of Touil station, and, looking ahead to the right, I saw the ditch. I climbed down into it and then up the slope on the other side. When I got to the top, I was out of breath, and right away I saw a little house partway down the hill, with a high enclosure and hedge all around it. I started to run toward it without pausing to catch my breath. I heard a pack of dogs barking excitedly. No entryway through the enclosure could be seen. I started to make my way around it, looking for the door and finally found it on the side opposite from where I had come. It was a high wooden gate, the doors ajar. I could hear the dogs on the other side. I rang several times, but no one came out— there was only the ferocious barking of the dogs, as if they were hunting. Remembering that I wore the suit gave me a bit of courage and I pushed open the door to go in.

The expansive courtyard looked like an overgrown wildlife refuge, with trees obscuring the view. I caught only a few glimpses of the house located a few hundred meters away. The barking got dangerously closer. Then, between the gradually thinning trees, I saw the house, and to the west, in a wide-open space, a young woman in the middle of the dog pack. There was a mannequin thrown to the ground and torn to shreds; it was an exact replica of a toxic waste and hazardous products conveyor. The dogs began howling strangely, cowering and huddling behind their master, who looked all around in concern. When I got close to her, the dogs were shaking and chomping their teeth so much that I might have been in a coffeehouse with a hundred waiters all suffering from Parkinson's disease!

"Good evening! Are you Vala?"

She turned around looking everywhere, scared to death.
"My God! What is it?"

I suddenly remembered the effects of Solima's suit and popped off the hood. The dogs' master had her back to me, scanning the other direction.

"Are you Vala?"

She yelled and whipped around on her heels to look in my direction, then let out a long shriek, raising her arms and spreading her hands wide, and jumped back, falling backwards into the middle of her dogs. She remained motionless, unconscious. I was flooded with remorse—I should have taken off the suit before coming in. I took it off before taking the young woman in my arms. I sat down far from the dogs and held her in my lap, gently tapping her cheeks.

"Wake up! I'm really sorry! I must have scared you— I'm so sorry! I had forgotten about Solima's nano-antennnas!"

When she opened her eyes, she pushed me away and stood up.

"Who are you? What are you doing here? Your face looks like the one I saw floating in mid-air with no body!"

I told her about the suit, but she didn't believe me, so I had to show her several times, putting on and taking off the suit several times before she calmed down a bit. Her dogs were still just as frightened.

"Those poor dogs," she said. "I have never seen them in such a pitiful state. I didn't think they could get this scared! And here I was counting on them to scare off intruders! But you, you must be an earthquake or some such phenomenon!"

I told her about the N'madi, but she didn't know who he was.

"He said that you were together in Windcity and that before his conviction you had already moved here. He said that he wrote to warn you when he got arrested."

"I'll go find his letter. For now, go wait for me in the house. Excuse me for a moment while I try to calm the dogs down."

I crossed the threshold with difficulty because of birds of all kinds coming in and out. The interior was even messier than the courtyard; it was like a greenhouse or the store in a park: very beautiful and very picturesque: birds, plants of all species and of all seasons which climbed or crawled, sometimes intertwining; fragrant flowers, stones of all sizes and colors and numerous small animals roaming around, including a pyramid rat and a wild field mouse arguing fiercely. I managed to make my way between the plants to sit on a chair I saw.

As dusk came on, the birds became more and more agitated, chirping and flying around in circles, sometimes bumping into the ceiling and knocking down the highest perches on the overhead beams. When she came back into the house, she found me sitting there, still just as uncomfortable, trying to find a good position so as not to damage a plant or crush one of the many critters swarming under the chair. She motioned to me with a jerk of her head.

"Come on, we're going upstairs!"

We took a little wooden spiral staircase that I hadn't seen before. She had me sit down in a bare-walled rectangular room with a few monitors and a lot of books and cushions scattered about on the floor. I settled down on a cushion covered in animal hair and started to sneeze uncontrollably. Without a sound, she served me a hot, fragrant drink with fresh green leaves floating on top.

"I'm sorry for my intrusion, but I didn't know where to go."

And since she didn't answer, I went on, slightly embarrassed.

"I'm all alone in the world! I have no one, you know..."

"You don't have any parents or friends?"

"I have no one!"

"And this Solima who helped you escape?"

"Oh, her! You wouldn't even believe it! I don't even know why I say 'her,' for she isn't a woman- she isn't even a human being. She only took on the appearance of a woman to be able to communicate with humans... She's a vampire who feeds on spoken words! She went to Mars to shift her shape and take on a human form... No, she's not a person— she's a vampire who travels in a black hole and all over the Milky Way!"

"And your parents? What happened to them?"

"My parents? I never had any! I was born just as you see me! I opened my eyes for the first time not that long ago, on top of the cliff overlooking the Imdel Facility!"

I think that from that moment on she gave up trying to untangle my enigma and lumped the absurdity of my existence in with the absurdity of hers, accepting me just as I was. She decided to forget my bizarre side.

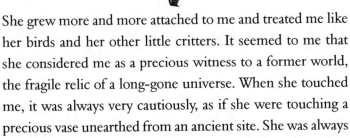

She grew more and more attached to me and treated me like her birds and her other little critters. It seemed to me that she considered me as a precious witness to a former world, the fragile relic of a long-gone universe. When she touched me, it was always very cautiously, as if she were touching a precious vase unearthed from an ancient site. She was always sad and often cried for no reason. Sometimes she was gone for several long weeks, leaving me alone in the house to take care of the plants and animals. In the evenings, I read her poetry collections about nature, which made me feel her presence and hear her voice. She had always had a boundless passion for nature, and it was this passion that drove her to leave Windcity.

She hated Windcity and I also came to hate this city that she described to me so many times:

"Imagine a city wrapped in a thick veil of irradiated dust, loaded with destructive emissions that tinge the daylight with a sickly grayish-yellow. A city with no planning or architecture, where each man claimed his spot and built a shelter or a palace, outdoing each other in bad taste. A city whose labyrinth of streets, always sandy and dusty, are often blocked by piles of garbage, or by pets, donkeys, goats, sheep, camels, and cows that roam free—sometimes by their corpses in a state of decomposition, several days after their death, poisoned by the toxic waste they feed on in the public landfills, or run over by a passing vehicle. If it weren't for the mounds of garbage encircling the city and wafting its fetid odor all the way across the ocean, Windcity would have long ago been swallowed up by the sand.

"Men, beasts, and machines swarm everywhere searching for their daily subsistence. Occasionally, here and there, a sudden and inexplicable death—a beast or a person, by accident or in a vehicle stuck in a sand-clogged road— brings a brutal stop to their mad wanderings. A cadaver, an abandoned or broken-down vehicle, a mob, a skirmish, a brawl, or a fight will block the path of the wandering things and beings, but very soon, the bottleneck will disperse and the flux of becoming will resume its infernal race.

"As night falls, the clamor subsides; the air cools off and clears up. The dark streets are lit by the headlights of rattletraps as well as luxury sedans captivated by the haunting twinkle in the eyes of the ladies of the night. Drug and potassium iodide deals flourish at night. Drugs help to console yourself from being born and to forget the miseries of the just-finished day and to take your mind off those to come tomorrow. As for the potassium, it helps those who, clinging desperately to life, want to survive the effects of radioactivity for a few more years or days, no matter the cost. The directors of the National Office of Preventative Health (NOPH), a publicly-funded establishment created to provide the citizens of the Republic of Barzakh with the products necessary to counteract the effects of radioactivity, set aside the majority of their supplies to keep the black market going. Every moment of the day, long lines of men, women and children seeking their daily dose of potassium can be seen in front of the NOPH offices, which are found in every neighborhood of Windcity. Small quantities will be distributed to a few of the privileged and to those who've assured the services of an agent by corrupting him. To the others, they will announce that supplies have run out, that there will be no more available that day and that they might as well go try another office. The sale of potassium is illegal, since the NOPH is supposed to have a monopoly on the free distribution of sufficient quantities of the product. In reality, those who want their daily dose are often forced to pay outrageous prices for it on the black market that is tightly controlled by Tangalla himself.

"In Windcity, inequality and injustice are on display at every turn. The cash brought in by the international landfills for toxic waste and hazardous products only profit Tangalla and his clan. The gaping abyss between the rich and the poor grows wider every day. In the northwest, near the seaside road, the residential neighborhood—made up of embassies, luxurious villas belonging to courtiers, and hotels, all grouped around Tangalla's palace—is but a minuscule section of the immense shanty town that extends toward the north, east, south, and southwest for dozens of kilometers. Hundreds of thousands of filthy huts are thrown together any which way, and more appear each day, slowly taking over the public dumping grounds. Abnormally high levels of radioactive pollution are always found in the vicinity of the port, where the toxic waste and hazardous products destined for the various storage facilities are unloaded."

She told me about her bitter disappointment, when, after spending a night watching the stars emerge and die away, the pallid glow of dawn blotted them out and cast its light on the vast multitudes of crumbling houses in Windcity.

"What a contrast," she said, "between the glorious beauty of the celestial vastness and those low structures, so striking in their ugliness and disorder. Faced with the sight of that city, which at times resembles an ugly prostitute whose heavy makeup has gotten smeared during the night, the same depressing question kept tormenting my mind: What's the point of the human species?"

One night, as I slept next to her, I was awoken by the sound of her crying. I urgently asked her why she was crying. That's when she told me, for the first time, about her child who was still there….

"I would do anything, no matter how crazy, to save my child!"

When she said this last part, her voice sounded oddly tragic, as if she had had a premonition of a great misfortune.

Save the Sahara

We often watched holovision, especially in the evenings before going to bed. One such evening, just after she had returned home from one of her long absences, we were watching the news. The first part of the broadcast was devoted, as usual, to coverage of Tangalla's every movement and deed, opening with images of Tangalla welcoming the CEO of RSRW International, a global corporation in charge of reprocessing and storing radioactive waste.

Vala couldn't help but exclaim, "Look at that! He's all smiles with that pig. No doubt he's begging for a new sub-vention for one of his facilities!"

A voice-over commentated the images from the ceremony.

"...with whom our country maintains a sincere and fruitful cooperation. Speaking of which, we remind you that emissaries from RSRW International recently visited our Eastern Hodh province where they promised to build new storage facilities and a reprocessing factory."

The broadcast cut back to the presenter, whose thick

makeup failed to hide his exhausted and swollen face. His eyes glued to the teleprompter, he read the news with forced energy—indifferent to the comedy as well as the tragedy of the events he was relating.

"In Eastern Hodh, 'Save the Sahara' claimed responsibility for yesterday's attack on trucks transporting material earmarked for the construction of a storage facility in that region. We remind you that five conveyors were killed in this attack and that a significant amount of material was destroyed— the cost of the damage was estimated at 25 million ouguiyas. The guerrilla fighters of the 'Save the Sahara' movement are generally recruited among the N'madis, that ancient tribe of former nomads who subsisted by hunting addax antelopes in the Great Desert. The terrorists use the same methods as their ancestors, but instead of training their Sloughi dogs to hunt the now extinct addax, they target conveyors, so easy to spot driving their big red trucks, wearing their white suits and protective masks. The terrorists operate all along the main highway used by the conveyors to transport waste toward the storage facilities in the Great Desert. But attacks occur most often on the stretch between Tamoukret and Awana.

"And now for science news. A team from the Institute of Geophysics reported that global warming is causing the carbon dioxide currently present in sedimentary rocks in the form of carbonates to leak out and dissipate into the atmosphere. If this phenomenon continues to increase, the oceans will boil and the Earth will become the Devil's cauldron..."

I was awoken by Vala. She had switched on the light

and was shaking all over. She was soaking wet and told me that she had just had a horrible nightmare.

"I was in a deep, fitful sleep filled with nightmares and strange dreams. And then, a monster appeared with Tangalla. He lit a huge fire at the foot of our bed. He had a frail neck, a lean, even bony face, red eyes, a narrow, wrinkled forehead, a flat nose, a huge mouth, swollen lips, a short and tapered chin, a goatee, and straight pointed ears, straight and messy hair, fanged teeth, a cone-shaped occiput, humped chest and back, and sordid clothing. He blew on the fire and thrashed about furiously, waving a whip over Tangalla, who, like a miserable naked slave, fed the fire under the cauldron. When the cauldron started to rumble, causing the lid to rattle wildly, the monster grabbed me, ripped off my clothes and threw me into it… It was awful! I will never be able to sleep again!"

I tried to calm her down a bit, but she kept wailing.

"We are threatened by terrible catastrophes, yet we are doing nothing. The ever-increasing global warming is devastating; it will force us to exile ourselves from Earth, as Adam from Heaven. Humanity will embark on a new eternity of wandering and will only have a telescopic view of Earth, like the one we have of Venus. Our Earth today is a dying world where life is no longer able to tolerate the excesses, injustice, and arrogance of man. No life can resist the hazards of chemical and nuclear pollution, desertification, overpopulation, and shortages of food and water. Man has fashioned the Earth—he has made this planet what it is by blindly and thoughtlessly altering the earthly environment for his personal convenience, with a view to short-term

199

economic profit rather than for the long-term benefit of its inhabitants. The layer of pollution, carbon dioxide, and water vapor that has formed around the Earth makes the atmosphere so thick that the majority of infrared thermal emissions can't escape into space. This overheating effect will raise the temperature of the Earth's surface to 400°C and higher. Our planet will become the devil's cauldron. And those responsible for this situation have abandoned Earth and left us here, forbidding us to leave this hellscape...."

I knew she was right to be worried. Faced with her extreme distress, I tried to make her see a glimmer of hope.

"You are right; life on Earth is no longer possible! But there are other, more promising places in the solar system and elsewhere... Of course, there are security barriers around the Earth and visas are more and more difficult to obtain, but I'm sure that one day, you and I will be able to leave this old Earth for good and settle down under more favorable skies, colonizing lunar deserts and picnicking on the ancient shores of Mars or in celestial forests. Or maybe we'll go on an adventure to faraway galactic megacities..."

"You know perfectly well that all these plans are crazy! We live in an environment that is saturated with chemical and nuclear pollution; our life expectancy is nothing and we're not allowed to make plans!"

Moved by her despair, I blurted out, "We could try to do something and not remain passive..."

"That's just what I was going to say! My dogs are ready now. I have been training them for a long time to hunt the toxic waste and hazardous products conveyors!"

The deadly dawn caught us discussing the location of our first operation.

A few days later, we were at Cheggat with our dogs. We had located our prey more than five kilometers from the attack site—a big cargo truck that was still parked in the rest area. After identifying our target, we split up. We each went to one side of the highway, followed by our pack of Sloughi dogs, alert and obedient. We hid ourselves in the bordering dune fields. Behind me on both sides, the dogs, quiet as mice, kept their eyes glued on my hands, ready to execute the maneuver they were trained for the moment I gave the signal. When the truck came abreast of us, our voices rang out as one across the desert, *"Alehgou! Alehgou! Wouch! Wouch!"* and we bolted after our barking dogs as they pursued the truck, which sped up in an attempt to escape the ferocious pack. But the dogs were already surrounding it, on the hood, clinging to both sides of the cab, their snarling jaws full of sharp fangs pressing furiously against the windshield and cab windows. Other dogs sunk their fangs into the tires, bursting and shredding them. The truck finally came to a stop, but not before running over a few dogs, who let out long, piercing, broken cries as they lay dying.

The conveyors had taken out their weapons, but they stayed barricaded in the cab. I grabbed a big rock and threw it against the windshield, shattering it into a thousand pieces. Then the conveyors opened fire. I was wounded, but several dogs succeeded in breaching the cab. They were biting the conveyors, dragging them out of the cab across the hood and dropping heavily onto the bloody asphalt with their prey... I saw flying machines swooping down on us, shooting rockets that exploded as they hit the ground. I dove onto Vala and rolled under the truck, pulling her with me. The dogs were exterminated. We were tied up and transported to the Aghreijit garrison.

On the first day at Aghreijit, two perfectly anonymous people wearing dark glasses and carrying black suitcases stuffed with files came to visit me in my cell. They introduced themselves as my lawyer and a representative from the Prisoner Aid Agency, giving me several complicated forms to fill out, starting with puzzling questions such as "first and last name," "father's name," "mother's name," "date and place of birth," etc. Then for a long time, burly and intimidating investigators came several times a day to threaten me and ask me the same unanswerable questions: "Who are you?" "Where do you come from?" "What are your motives?" etc. The representative from Prisoner Aid Agency said that I couldn't go to court without filling out the forms.

I received no news of Vala, until one day I got a letter from her that left me speechless. She informed me that she was in Windcity and had "managed to win Tangalla's heart, who was now speaking of marriage more and more often"!

It's crazy how well women master the art of adapting themselves and building new relationships. In the same letter, she said that the perspective of marriage didn't particularly thrill her, but when the moment came, she would say yes, for her son who would benefit greatly from her new situation. Then she confessed her remorse to me. She said that her survival instinct and her egoism tortured her conscience; she also said that she doubted that her love for her son was a valid justification for her relationship with a polluter and an assassin, and admitted that only human cowardice and corruption could explain her submissiveness.

Soon, I got a visit from the lawyer who came to inform me that the judge had decided to hold my trial without waiting for the forms. He advised me to confess my identity if I wanted to get off easy. So, he didn't believe me either, even though I kept telling him endlessly, "I don't know who I am."

Then I got another letter from Vala in which she told me that her marriage to Tangalla would be celebrated at the beginning of winter. And from then on, I could think of nothing else.

I appeared in court, indifferent to what sentence they would give me. They accused me of all sorts of crimes, calling me a "dangerous mercenary from a foreign land," a "highly trained spy," a "terrorist who took advantage of a trusting woman's hospitality," etc. When the verdict was announced, I was not surprised:

"… Consequently, you are condemned to be deprived of water until death ensues! The sentence will be carried out at Ghallawiya."

I found myself on top of the mountain, abandoned to die of thirst, surrounded by a double row of security guards who were relieved every hour. My thoughts kept returning to what Vala and Tangalla's wedding would be like after my death.

For seven days, the citizens of Barzakh will hold festivities to celebrate the marriage of their President. There will be congratulatory messages and telegrams from all over the world. But the weather will not cooperate—a violent sandstorm will rage for two months, day and night, without interruption, as it does at the beginning of every winter, and the air will be saturated with noxious grayish-yellow dust. But this will not keep the Barzakhians from dancing and singing from the depths of their radioactive dust-filled throats, and eating dishes seasoned with sand, gritty between their teeth.

One week before the wedding, Vala will be delivered to the blacksmith women who, in the Barzakhian tradition, take care of preparing the bride. They will fix her hair, apply her henna, dress her, and put on her makeup, with attendants to prepare the tea. They will exchange gossip and force-feed the bride obscene stories to arouse her and get her ready for her wedding night.

During the entire time of preparation, Vala will feel like a cadaver being prepared for burial. Yet, bustling around her like a swarm of bees, the smith women will be merry—some speaking in loud voices, others laughing uproariously. Some will be fussing over the bride's hair, dyeing one section, braiding or rubbing pomade into another section. Others will take hold of her feet and hands, on which they will form complicated arabesques with tape, meticulously carving the designs with thin razor blades. Others will periodically press large chunks of ice to her hands and feet to keep them from sweating, so that the adhesive will stick well. These same women will mix and shape the dark blue smooth henna paste destined for her hands and feet, which will then be wrapped in plastic, like mummies, for forty-eight hours.

In each corner of the room, the faint smoke from the perfume-warmers will rise toward the ceiling like the souls of enchanted spirits who were punished and imprisoned for centuries inside a bottle lost in the depths of the oceans, and who were liberated one day by a providential hand. Virgins will lift the bride's veils to slip little smoking incense burners underneath. The stifling room will be permeated by a strong odor composed of a mixture of fragrant wood, precious powder, perfumed adhesive, balsam spurge leaves, and perfumes, which will make their heads spin, intoxicating their senses and freeing them from that eternal dependence upon oxygen.

They will also prepare the new veil that the bride will wear on her wedding night—two pieces of delicate, sheer, indigo black fabric, five meters long and eighty-five centimeters wide that have been sewn together. For the entire week leading up to the wedding, this veil will be sprayed with perfume, imbued with incense, and sprinkled with Tidikt powder, then tightly knotted and rolled up into a ball and wrapped in plastic so it will soak up as much fragrance as possible. The bride's hair will be drawn into a glorious bun in the front of her head to hold the veil in place. The hairdressers will adorn it with jewels of gold, pearls, and shells. When her hands and feet are finally unwrapped, delicate strips of wood held in the capable hands of the smith women will gently scrape off the smooth, consistent paste of the slightly dried-out henna and peel off the arabesques of tape, revealing the magnificent golden-red decorations and the radiance of the ideal beautiful figure, full of sensuality, unifying the henna's artistic design.

To celebrate the blossoming of this beauty, they will slip rings on her fingers—delicate golden rings of various shapes, engraved with magic grids combining Chinese, Japanese, or perhaps Babylonian-inspired letters and numbers. Her hands will slip into bracelets of ebony and silver, and her feet into anklets that will jingle each time the bride moves or crosses her legs, creating a throbbing reverberation of desire across the unfathomable abyss of voluptuousness. The veil soaked in aphrodisiac perfumes will be unfurled and attached to her shoulders by smooth round fibula brooches carved out of shells. On her chest, her breasts will catch the tumbling pearl necklace composed of triangles of carnelian and little pearls of glass, stone, and amber— square-cut and set in the traditional way. Forming the central pendant, a very light plate of gold will hold little soldered cylinders, crowned with a half-sphere and a pocket woven out of golden thread and forming a sort of horn of plenty, from which will emerge tiny golden huts placed on scalloped bowls. These designs affixed by a hook-shaped golden thread will be separated from the central design by orbs of carnelian. Another necklace of cloves will be sewn into the veil along the neckline, the string of cloves will be separated by bits of precious wood. Her long black hair, laden with pearls, will cascade across her chest, over her shoulders, and down her back. Through it, one will be able to glimpse golden hoops, encrusted with Amazonite pearls, attached to the upper ear or dangling from the earlobes.

I imagined her learning of my death, glancing distractedly at the newspaper resting on the edge of her breakfast platter and finding a photo of my bare head in full sun on the front page, followed immediately by a snapshot of my cadaver covered in dust and surrounded by armed soldiers. I imagined her reading the captions that will say, "To the end, he refused to reveal his identity," or "What were his last thoughts?" Another photo will show a close-up of my head tilting back, almost ecstatic, under which the captions will read anything from "It is all over," to "Justice is served" or "All that remains is silence."

Perhaps she won't see me until much later, when I am nothing more than a cadaver in the last stages of decomposition or a skeleton almost entirely picked clean of flesh (except perhaps a few shreds that will still be hanging on). But most likely, she will never see me again except as an anonymous skull with exaggerated eye sockets, on display behind glass in some museum.

But atony already pushes away all these thoughts. Memories of Vala gave way to a profound fear, a dreadful anguish and a ferocious hatred of the human species. Each passing hour was torture for my body doomed to hunger and thirst, which abated at night only to make the trial more cruel the next day. Suffering gradually took over the entire body, like quicksand. My lips, mouth, and throat dried out and cracked. My stomach and intestines tightened up and were twisted by a prodigious force, as if it were wringing the last drops of liquid from them. A raging fire burned my entrails, the blaze then spreading up to my face, hands, and chest. Atrocious pain radiated throughout my entire body, getting worse over time, in sudden bursts, followed by slow lulls. My head and brain were painfully compressed by a powerful vice, and violent fits of fever racked my body, beginning with severe shivering, then despondency, then gradual euphoria. The intense pain eased up, the spasms stopped, and my legs stretched out. My panting, exhausted flesh no longer needs anything, no longer suffers, no longer feels hunger or thirst. I hear buzzing sounds, impressions of chloroform through long sound waves. I was in a new world, where insignificant and bizarre memories of my departing life besieged me like vultures. As life was about to leave me, I felt like I was pulling away from my own body. At the same moment, a luminous tunnel appeared to me, and all my past life unfolded before my eyes. I had the feeling of reliving it. I witnessed it as a total stranger this time…

The transcriptions were filed in the Archaeological Institute of Human Thought's public library under the reference code: "Death throes of a man from Barzakh, 1034-2057 (?)"

About the Author

Moussa Ould Ebnou, one of Mauritania's greatest novelists, earned his Ph.D. at the Sorbonne in Paris, France, and is a philosophy professor at the University of Nouakchott in Mauritania. He has written several novels and short stories in French and Arabic. He was a consultant for the United Nations Sudano-Sahelian Office in New York and served as a cultural advisor to the Presidency of Mauritania for fifteen years.